A

DENIABLE

ASSET

JOHN MACRAE-HALL

IUNIVERSE, INC.
BLOOMINGTON

A Deniable Asset

iUniverse books may be ordered through booksellers or by contacting:

iUniverse
1663 Liberty Drive
Bloomington, IN 47403
www.iuniverse.com
1-800-Authors (1-800-288-4677)

ISBN: 978-1-4502-8078-5 (sc)
ISBN: 978-1-4502-8079-2 (dj)
ISBN: 978-1-4502-8080-8 (ebk)

Library of Congress Control Number: 2010918821

Printed in the United States of America

iUniverse rev. date: 2/15/2011

PROLOGUE

July 21, 1947. Derby Flying Club, Burnaston Airfield, England.

The Auster J4 turned into the prevailing wind, and the pilot, Harry, having run through the short before-takeoff checklist, said to his young passenger in the right-hand seat, "Okay, Johnny, why don't you just rest your hands and feet on the controls and follow me through the takeoff?"

As he gently opened the throttle, the Cirrus Minor four-cylinder engine revved up to its full power at 2,600 rpm, and the small three-seat aircraft slowly began to accelerate across the smooth grass field, setting in motion a chain of events that would profoundly direct the future life of young John.

As the aircraft accelerated, John felt the first delicate tugs of airflow over the rudder, ailerons, and elevators, feeding back through the control runs to his fingertips. All he had read and dreamt about before became clear in an instant; this was the transition of theory and imagination into reality. Almost unconsciously he eased the control column forward a minute amount, and the aircraft responded by lifting its tail as the airflow increased over the flying surfaces. As the tail rose, the horizon became more apparent over the engine cowling, the speed approached sixty knots, the aircraft bounced gently, once, twice, and applying an almost instinctive whisper of backward pressure on the control column, John felt the aircraft leave the ground. The left wing dropped a little, and, again, instinctively, he applied corrective action with a touch or rudder and aileron.

The climb continued to two thousand feet, and Harry said, "Right now! We'll try a few turns." As the aircraft banked to the left, it felt as though it was skidding sideways. Something in John's memory cells remembered, *Balance the slip in the turn with rudder.* A gentle pressure on the left rudder corrected the feeling of imbalance, and the horizon gently and smoothly rotated.

The flight progressed through all the basic manoeuvres, turns, climbs, descents, and a gentle demonstration of a stall and recovery. As one manoeuvre followed another, John's unconscious learning curve grew at an exponential rate. It was as though a five-finger exercise on a piano was growing into a concerto, everything felt so magical; it was as though he had become one with the aircraft.

"Well," said Harry, "let's go back to the field and try a landing." John sensed that they needed about a sixty-degree turn to the right to do so, and simply by looking that way, the Auster seemed to sense his intention. It turned, and the airfield appeared on the near horizon. Harry then talked their way through a circuit and landing, and John followed through on the controls accordingly. As the aircraft neared the ground, he felt the right moment to ease back on the control column to check the rate of descent, and the Auster settled gently on the ground, with just one small bounce, as Harry pulled off the power.

They taxied back to the dispersal area and went through the shutdown procedure. Whilst walking back to the clubhouse, Harry said, "What did you think to all of that then, Johnny?" Johnny replied enthusiastically, "That was the best thing that I can ever remember doing! You made it all look so easy," little realising it was he who had done it all.

A flight with the CFI—a retired RAF flight instructor—followed, and John's natural ability made a profound impression upon him. He later confided to Harry, "I've never seen anything like it; he can fly it better than I can, Harry!"

John's future and his part in the great events of the Cold War, with all its intrigue, lay ahead. The die was cast.

ONE

This was John Malcolm Frazer's fifteenth birthday, and the big surprise of the day had been when, shortly after breakfast, Harry had arrived and announced that if he, Johnny, had nothing more important to do, they would go flying. John jumped at the chance.

Nineteen forty-seven in postwar Britain was a curious time. A massive feeling of exuberance had followed the titanic events of World War II. D-day and victory in Europe arrived; total victory would follow. The dark clouds had passed, and the forthcoming defeat of Japan seemed a foregone conclusion. Winston Churchill, the prime minister, had nursed the nation through the conflict and had inspired not only Great Britain but the rest of the free world as well. Being a truly great man, he had not clung to power, as many would have done; being the great parliamentary figure he was, he sensed the mood of the nation, that it was now time to disband the national government and go to the nation by holding an election so they might have a government of popular choice. An overwhelming majority had returned the Labour Party, led by Clement Attlee, and a Socialist government was installed. At the time, few realized just what a disastrous mistake had occurred. By 1947, the precious hopes and dreams of peace and prosperity had faded fast, and the dull realization of the heavy yoke of Socialism was beginning to be felt by the nation. Nonetheless, the spirit of enterprise still flourished in the hearts of many; among them was Harry and many of his friends.

The entrepreneurs of the day, the small businessmen who had not been nationalised, had flourished surprisingly, even with all the shortages, rationing, and difficulties that prevailed. Harry had been fortunate and sound in his judgment; his garage business in the small town of Measham in Derbyshire had grown considerably. With the shortage of new cars, the business of buying, repairing, and selling older cars had become a very profitable pursuit as the nation slowly began to revive. As a part of one deal, involving several vehicles, an aircraft had been included. This was the Auster J4, almost brand new, one of a batch manufactured by the Auster Aircraft Limited Company at Rearsby, quite nearby in Leicestershire.

Harry was a great friend of John's parents and had unconsciously become his mentor. He was a dashing figure, always well dressed and groomed, sporting a generous moustache and a trim Vandyke beard. Very personable and a good storyteller, he presented the spirit of success in an otherwise drab and cheerless country where depression and crisis were, currently, the order of the day. Individualism and free enterprise were frowned upon by a Labour government whose main achievement had been one crisis after another and whose policy seemed to be that of "misery shared."

When John had returned home that evening, he glowed with the thrill of the day. He basked in the spotlight as Harry recounted the events of the flight and the considerable talent his novice pilot had displayed. This was a rare occurrence in John's day-to-day existence. Throughout the recently ended World War II, he had avidly followed the exploits of all branches of the military and had yearned to be able to play some part. He dreamt of being a pilot in the Royal Air Force. To this end he had assiduously studied, with great zeal, vast amounts of technical information on ships and aircraft and their operation, in concert with so many of his schoolboy friends of those days. Now it had all come into focus; the events of this day and his joy at discovering his innate ability to fly an aircraft put all other lingering doubts aside. He knew his destiny was to be a Royal Air Force pilot.

The previous year, 1946, on the fifth of March, Winston Churchill had delivered his famous "Iron Curtain" speech at Fulton in the United

States. This speech laid before the world the stark realization that the gigantic events of World War II had not rid the world of terror. An even darker and more sinister threat to the peace of the world had arisen. The Soviet Union, under Stalin, had made obvious to the world at large its ultimate aim of world domination. Peace, as they portrayed it, would only be possible when a Communist government, under the thrall and guidance of the USSR, governed every country and nation in the world. Now, in Britain, the hopes for a peaceful future faded only to give way to the certainty that a long and protracted struggle lay ahead. There were deep divisions politically. By 1947, the gilded promises of the Socialist government had given way to stark reality.

Rationing was stricter than during wartime; the country was deeply in debt, and industrial strife abounded within industry. Almost monthly, the government announced a new "crisis," and its popularity dwindled by the day. Far from the hopes of a peaceful future, the Cold War had begun, with all the sinister import that title implied.

To counteract this threat, the NATO alliance was born to counter the risk that the Soviet Union, having already taken over all of Eastern Europe after VE day, would begin an assault upon Western Europe as the first part in its plan for world domination. Britain, Belgium, Denmark, France, Iceland, Italy, Luxemburg, The Netherlands, Norway, and Portugal, also Canada and the United States, committed themselves to come to each other's defence in the event of a military attack upon any one of them. Thus, the battle line was drawn. It gave a clear signal to the USSR that another world conflict would ensue should they venture upon a course of aggression.

The Soviets thereupon continued to pursue, with even greater vigour, a policy of aggression by every other means, short of war, against the western allies. They embarked on a programme of social unrest, dislocation of industry by taking control of trade unions and causing strikes and walkouts, undermining morale by propaganda in the press and media, political indoctrination of young people through the influence of their fellow travellers in education, and economic warfare on a hitherto unparalleled scale.

Complete demobilisation of the British armed forces had been impossible to achieve, and, in fact, an expansion of the forces was beginning. Keen as he was, John would have to wait for two years to

3

pass before he was able to join the Royal Air Force. As it was, there was not a local air training corps unit in his local town, Tamworth; however, there was an army cadet unit at his school, which he promptly joined in order to commence some form of initial military training. He reasoned that whichever branch of the military one was a part of, the disciplines would be similar, and, above all else, one should be able to use small arms to some effect. Furthermore, ground training and fieldwork would always be useful.

He had received some training of this nature in the Boy Scouts, but his best tutor had been his friend, a local poacher of some renown, who rejoiced in the nickname of "Fudge." Under his guiding hand, John learned many nocturnal and twilight skills of silent movement, use of natural cover, stealth, concealment, and stalking, animal lore, and, perhaps above all, a real sense of situational awareness essential to the well-being of any successful poacher. The gamekeepers they evaded were a highly skilled bunch who, curiously, had grown to admire Fudge's skill, artistry, and sheer animal cunning. In the foxhunting shires of the Midlands of England, these were highly respected accomplishments, and those individuals who possessed them to any degree were highly regarded by the local population.

In this respect, John was something of an oddity. He had been born in the city of Birmingham. When he was two years of age, his father died. His mother, a strong and determined businesswoman, decided that it would be best for him to live in the loving care of his paternal grandparents, who lived nearby. They were a comfortably situated family, his grandfather being a retired merchant businessman, living in a large house in a quiet suburb on the southern side of the city. From a very early age, John had shown an avid interest in all things mechanical. At the age of three, whilst on a family holiday at the seaside, he rode for the first time on a fairground roundabout. His first mount was upon a wooden horse. This did not suit him; he wanted to try out the small car. That ride satisfied, he then insisted on a ride in the aeroplane. During the ride, he tugged hard on the dummy control wheel, getting more agitated by the minute. At the end of the ride, a frustrated and tearful child was complaining bitterly that the aeroplane would not fly!

When he entered school at five years of age, he could already read fluently. His two favourite books were one about aeroplanes and the other about cars. These were not young children's books; they were for teenagers. The house had a detached garage, which contained his deceased father's two cars: an Austin 7 "Chummy" fabric-bodied saloon, and a rather lordly Delage D8 saloon of 1930 vintage. These fascinated young John, who at every opportunity could be found sitting inside them in the driver's seat, trying to peer over the wheel and making imaginary "driving noises." One day, he discovered the driver's handbook for the little Austin in a side pocket on the door. With the book were also the keys. The now six-year-old boy avidly read the handbook, familiarising himself with all the controls. To him the way seemed clear; he turned on the ignition switch, pulled out the choke, and pressed the starter button, and the engine started. He climbed out of the car, opened the garage doors, climbed back in again, declutched, and put the gear lever into reverse. Releasing the handbrake and applying just a touch of power, he eased in the clutch. Now, the clutch is a very sensitive thing on an Austin 7; it is of the "sudden death" variety. Total pedal movement between out and fully engaged is about one quarter of an inch and is the most challenging control to operate properly on the vehicle. The results of John's first attempt were predictable; the little car was either going to stall or reverse quite rapidly. It did the latter. It jerked backwards. In doing so, John lurched forward, and his foot went hard down on the accelerator. The very lightly laden car shot out of the garage in reverse and totally out of control, went down the driveway, crashed into the closed gate, destroying it, then traveled across the footpath and out onto the roadway, where it finally stalled, leaving its shaken and now tearful operator pondering his fate. Happily, there was no other traffic passing; a total disaster was avoided, and the garage was barred and bolted until the cars had gone.

Being the only child in a household did not seem to trouble him. He had one very good friend, a neighbour's son named Phillip. Together they shared many boyhood dreams. His mother subsequently had remarried just after the outbreak of World War II. Her new husband was a countryman from a small village between Tamworth, in Staffordshire, and Ashby-De-La-Zouch, in Leicestershire. They had brought the village inn, named The Four Counties, and taken residence there. John remained at his school in the city during the week and travelled out to the village at weekends and holiday times.

His grandfather had become chief of the civil defence organization, known as the ARP, in their sector of the city at the outbreak of hostilities. When air raids began, he would walk to the control centre nearby and, after checking in all the wardens, would go out on patrol himself, normally accompanied by young John. It was easy to see where there was trouble. Bomb bursts would give a very clear indication. They would hurry to the site and direct any ARP personnel on the spot to extinguish any small fires that had started and then immediately begin to check for survivors. Leaving a man in charge of the site, they would then move on to the next area and so on until the all-clear siren. Immediately then began first aid treatment of the injured and the rescue of survivors trapped in fallen buildings. Quite often, youngsters of John's age would assist, going into the ruins where a grown man could not to listen for anyone trapped who may be conscious but dazed and disoriented. To boys of this ilk it was a great adventure and not particularly threatening. Curiously enough, grown men often drew strength from the boys' conduct, overcoming their own fears, phobias, and perturbations.

This type of exposure to danger gave John a certain gravity in his behaviour when faced by adversities. The village boys who tended to be larger and stronger did not possess his endurance, nimble-mindedness, and sophistication. After some initial attempts to bully, which failed miserably, they began to turn to him for a degree of leadership, which seemed to come naturally from him despite the fact that he was a somewhat shy and introverted boy for the most part.

Although slightly built, John was very agile and active. He was generally good at sports but tended to be an individualist as opposed to being a team player. He excelled at cricket, being in his school team and a player in the village team. Rugby was his favourite winter sport, where he shone as a wing three-quarter. His other great love was his bicycle, which provided him his primary means of transport. During the week, he rode to and from school and at weekends would ride out the twenty-five miles to the village on Friday afternoons, returning on to the city on Sundays.

His greatest interest was in motor vehicles of every type, aircraft, and ships. His favourite reading was technical books and adventure stories. During the long summer holidays, he worked with the local lads on farms. For the most part, horses were the major form of motive power.

The farm tractor was a somewhat rare machine in Britain in 1939, and, generally, only the larger farms possessed one. They became more abundant as the war progressed, and the younger farm hands joined the fighting services. The older men generally did not like tractors. They preferred horses, with which they were far more familiar. Young John revelled in their dislike of tractors. He understood every nut and bolt of their workings, and at ten years of age could drive one very competently; the horse brigade was happy to have him do so.

As a scholar, he puzzled his teachers; his school reports varied greatly from one subject to another. In some he excelled—geography, mechanical science, history, and languages were excellent, generally. In mathematics, he excelled with basics and mental configurations but lost interest in theory. He totally abandoned even trying to memorize formulae of any description after finding out he could look it up in a book and then apply it as necessary. In fact, anything that involved learning by rote he despised, and he simply became disinterested. His attention would wander during classes, to the dismay and disdain of several teachers. However, if he took an interest in any subject he would avidly pursue it until he was very familiar with it. Two subjects he was a master of were political and military history, with which he had grown up under the quiet tutelage of his grandfather. Slowly, for John, the next two years passed whilst he prepared for the next great day in his life.

TWO

Eleven thirty a.m. Monday, Jan. 23, 1950. The military recruiting office, Litchfield, Staffordshire.

John parked his bicycle and entered the office to find the sole occupant to be a smartly uniformed RAF flight sergeant seated behind the desk, who greeted him.

"Good morning, m'lad! What can we do for you today?"

"Well, sir, I've come to volunteer for the RAF. I did telephone the office last Friday, and they said there would be someone from the RAF here this morning," John replied.

"Well then, you're the one who called. I understand you want to be a pilot?"

"Yes, sir, can you help me?"

"Well, I'll certainly try. Have a seat, and let's get started."

The first question the flight sergeant asked was John's age. John replied that he was exactly seventeen and a half on Saturday past and that he understood that he was not eligible before that age. The flight sergeant replied that was the case and went on to explain that he would have to attend and pass an aircrew selection board. Then, if he was successful, he would have to serve a minimum of eight years. Further details followed, and the paperwork was completed. John was then informed that he would be contacted in due course; however not much would happen until he reached his eighteenth birthday.

Upon arrival at his home later that afternoon, his parents enquired where he had been. When told of his interview, they were amazed and somewhat shocked to discover that he had volunteered for eight years of service. After a short while, however they felt a touch of pride in the fact that this was the first real decision of his adult life, and what a very important one it was.

As the next few months passed, John became somewhat despondent. Each day he would eagerly scan the post and be sorely disappointed. In July, his eighteenth birthday passed, and still nothing. His hopes began to fade. One week later, returning from a journey into town, his mother informed him that he had some mail. There was a buff envelope inscribed with the impressive embellishment, O.H.M.S., "On His Majesty's Service."

With a hollow feeling in his stomach, dreading rejection, John read the magic content, which informed him that he would report to the Aircrew Selection Centre at RAF Hornchurch, southeast of London, on Sunday the fifteenth of October for his selection board, and that further instructions, including a travel warrant, would be forthcoming.

Time dragged by even more slowly for poor John, but in due course, according to the instructions, on Sunday the fifteenth, John found himself installed in a barrack block room at the well-known Battle of Britain Airfield in company with twenty-nine other hopefuls who comprised the intake for the coming week. They were a very mixed collection of young men from all walks of life. Some of the older ones were fresh from university, complete with degrees; a couple of RAF "brats" were from the RAF Apprentices School at RAF Halton. The latter revelled in their exalted position of being "old soldiers" and told horror stories of the life ahead for those who were selected and the even more dreadful fates for those who failed.

The following morning, the four-day process began—two days of stringent medical examinations and initial interviews, followed by two days of aptitude tests and examinations. By the second evening, the numbers in the room had decreased by almost half, many for physical reasons. After the last of the tests on that Thursday, the survivors returned to the barrack room in the evening with a sense of foreboding. The majority had wanted to be pilots, but some had expressed a desire to be a navigator/bomb aimer, engineer, or wireless operator/air gunner. Whatever their choice, their ultimate fate would be decided the following day, and the atmosphere was most subdued as they all settled in for the night.

The following day dragged by for John—a few administrative details accomplished in the morning and a final, short physical examination prior to his final interview at 1530 hours in the afternoon. Entering the interview room, he found a rather pleasant officer seated behind the desk, who asked him to take a seat. A few questions followed, most of which were a review of the previous interview, regarding his background, schooling and hobbies, his one previous flight in the Auster, etc. Then, the inevitable question: "Why do you want to be a pilot?"

Curiously, John had no prepared answer for this question. He pondered for a moment and then replied, "I know I can be a good one. I believe that this country is facing a long struggle in the years ahead to defend our way of life, and I want to play a part in it. I think I could be most useful as a fighter pilot, sir."

The interviewing officer looked down at his paperwork for what seemed to John to be an eternity; he then looked up directly at him, his expression softening, and said, "God knows, John, what the future may hold, but I do feel that you will make a very good one. I'm pleased to tell you that you have been selected for pilot training; let me be the first to congratulate you and wish you the best of luck in your training program. I do sincerely hope we shall meet again in the future."

John rose and, shaking the officer's hand, said, "Thank you, sir. I hope so too." Leaving the room, young John was in a state of shock as he walked over to the clerk's desk in the outer office. A corporal seated behind the desk said, "Here's a railway warrant for you, to get you home. The bus will leave at 0900 tomorrow morning for the station. There's another warrant for you to get you from there to RAF Cardington, where you will report for initial processing on the first of November."

He walked back to the barrack room—walking on air, in a daze, numb with so many emotions—tremendously surprised that he had come through it all with his every hope attained. Upon arrival there, he found all the others chattering away, telling of their individual fates. Most were despondent to a certain degree; some were very crestfallen. Immediately John was asked, "What did you get?" He replied, "Pilot!"

with a certain exuberance. One voice said, "Well done. I made it too!" This was from a university type who had some flight instruction with his university air squadron. Of the initial thirty eager applicants, only these two had made the grade.

John returned to his home the following day and met with his quietly anxious parents. Upon seeing them, he affected a crestfallen look, and they immediately hastened to commiserate. Almost bursting at the seams, John blurted out, "In fact, I passed, and, I'm going to be a pilot!" That evening it was "drinks all round" and a bottle of champagne to boot.

A few days later, at the aircrew selection centre, the CO was looking through the latest batch of reports and noted that one recruit had attained the best-ever recorded aptitude test for the pilot category. He took a long and close look at that particular folder and then annotated it, "This young man's progress should bear watching with interest! Frazer has some remarkable talents that should be carefully developed."

THREE

July 1951. RAF Thornhill, 5 FTS, Gwelo, Rhodesia. 0700 hours local time.

The Tiger Moth stood on the flight line. In the front seat sat the instructor, Flight Sergeant "Taff" Williams; in the rear seat sat Acting Pilot Officer John M. Frazer. In front of the aircraft, the ground crewman stood awaiting instructions from the pilot. John recited the "Before Starting Engine Checklist," pausing at "ignition switches on" to put his left hand out of the open cockpit onto the cowling below the small windscreen, feeling for the two small magneto switches, and moving them to the "on" position.

Then, continuing, he called the order, "Contact!" The ground crew airman swung the propeller down with a well-practiced heave, and the Gipsy-Major four-cylinder engine burst into life. John's first instructional flight with the RAF was about to begin.

After a careful briefing to John, Taff Williams began with a demonstration of taxiing. No brakes on the Tiger Moth, just a tailskid, no directional control except by "Stick into wind and rudder," then a burst of power to the engine to blow the tail around to the direction required. Takeoff followed, on the grass, after an all-clear green light from the runway controller. Just as Harry had done three years earlier, Taff said, "Follow me through on the controls."

The Tiger Moth quivered as John applied full power. He felt the aircraft come alive in his hands. This time it seemed different—the open cockpit, no forward visibility until the tail came up, and then the head of Taff in the front cockpit, and the top mainplane seemed to fill the horizon, but, most of all, the whole airframe of wood, metal, and canvas covering seemed to quiver with a life of its own. Every little gust of wind was felt and accommodated; the controls felt like an extension of his hands, feet, and whole body. Somehow, Taff's voice giving instructions seemed simply a background to the voice of the aircraft; it seemed to tell John, "Now! I want to fly!" At that moment, with gentle pressures from John, it gently lifted from the ground, responding to his touch like a violin responds to its player.

Two days later, after John's fourth hour of instruction, the flight instructors gathered together with the flight commander to discuss the progress of their pupils. When it came to Taff's turn, he said, "Well, sir, young Marshall is coming along nicely, but Johnny Frazer is really something else! You should fly with him sir, it is quite an experience. He could go solo now."

The following day, the flight commander did fly with John and at debrief said to him, "Well done, Johnny! That was very nice. If it were up to me, I would let you go solo now, but, as you know, the new regulation dictates that you must have ten hours of instruction before we can turn you loose upon an unsuspecting world!"

9 August 1951. Moffat Satellite Airfield, Gwelo, Rhodesia.

This was an all-grass airfield with a flying club used by the RAF for Tiger Moth training operations to keep them separate from the Harvard operations at Thornhill. It was his tenth hour of flying, and after one circuit and landing, Taff climbed out of the front cockpit, fastened the safety straps, and said to John, "Off you go then! One circuit and land. Taxi back here, and if I give you a thumbs-up, off you go for forty-five minutes. Okay? Don't break it!"

At the forty-hour point, the final check ride on the Tiger Moth took place. John sailed through with no qualms at all. If anything, he relished the opportunity to display his ability. In the assessment given by the chief flying instructor it was noted that "besides having a remarkable talent for basic flying, he also seems to have a photographic memory for objects on the ground. On his final solo cross-country, he described each turning point with a host of features and with remarkable accuracy.

We shall watch his progress through the next stage, on the Harvard, with great interest."

The Harvard trainer was an American aircraft built by the North American Aviation Company and known by them as the AT-6 Texan. It is probably the best-known advanced training aircraft ever built. Used by many air forces, it proved to be a reliable, tough aircraft, giving novice pilots a full appreciation of the problems they would face dealing with much more powerful, piston-engine, propeller-driven fighters. It was not foolproof to fly, but repaid good handling by its pilot with a great sense of satisfaction.

Fresh from the simple, dainty, and agile Tiger Moth, to John, the Harvard 2b seemed enormous. An all-metal structure powered by a large 550hp Pratt and Whitney R-1340 radial engine, a retractable undercarriage, wing flaps, tailwheel, brakes, and a fully glazed enclosed cockpit canopy, it was so very different. The front cockpit, where the student sat, was very roomy, in common with most American aircraft. An old, hoary joke told by many RAF pilots was, "To take evasive action in a Yankee aircraft, you get up and run around in the cockpit!" British fighter cockpits were uncommonly tight, to the point where the sides just below the canopy touched one's shoulders, and any pilot taller than five feet ten was very cramped and rather uncomfortable.

On the takeoff run, a fair touch of rudder was required to counteract swing, and visibility forward was very restricted by the large engine. Once the tail came up as the aircraft accelerated, everything seemed to smooth out. One sat high in the front cockpit, and the visibility was good. The sliding canopy was kept open for takeoff and landing, and in the Rhodesian climate, most pilots preferred to keep it open for most of their flying. The instructor sat in the rear cockpit with much-reduced forward visibility. John had no problem with this new experience; all the extra controls and sophistication seemed a natural progression, and he quickly began to enjoy all the nuances of the machine, in particular landing the aircraft. In those days, aircraft with a tailwheel were described as "conventional aircraft"; those with a nosewheel were called "tricycle layout aircraft." Landing a conventional aircraft could be done in two different ways. The easiest method was the straight approach to the runway and, after the "flare-out," to check the rate of descent. The aircraft was flown onto the runway in a level attitude, touching down on the two main landing wheels, throttling back engine power and, as the speed decreased, lowering the tailwheel onto the ground. This was a straightforward procedure and was relatively easy to accomplish; however, it did result in a longer ground run before the wheel brakes could be applied.

The alternative method is the "fighter" approach. This is a curved approach from the end of the downwind leg, which is closer to the runway threshold than that used for the straight-in approach. The approach path from the downwind position is curved all the way down to the touchdown point on the runway, and the aircraft is landed in a tail down attitude, ideally, with all three wheels touching the ground, softly, at the same instance, without a bounce. Power is reduced gently and evenly all through this approach, and landing and a much shorter landing run results. Also, the runway is in view throughout the approach and not obscured by the engine as it is on the final stages of a straight-in approach. It is a more difficult procedure to accomplish smoothly and was the one that John chose to perfect and use on every possible occasion; it seemed so logical. He was not always very successful!

Rhodesia was an ideal country for aircrew training, primarily because of the superb weather conditions. Except for a few days in the rainy season, the weather was generally wonderful. Clear blue skies with unlimited visibility and benign temperatures, given the fact that although only twenty degrees below the equator, the whole country sits on the Highveld some five thousand feet above sea level. During the late 1930s the British government, in one of its more rational moments, realized that the looming conflict of war against Germany would require a great many more pilots and other aircrew than could be trained in Britain under wartime conditions. They duly instituted the "Empire Air Training Scheme" (EATS) setting up training bases in Canada and Rhodesia. Later, from 1940–42, they also set up bases in Australia and the United States.

The airfield at Gwelo, known as RAF Thornhill, had been constructed in the remarkably short time of twelve weeks from the bare veldt in 1940. This included a dedicated railway siding to accept trains direct from Cape Town in South Africa. One hundred miles away to the southwest is the city of Bulawayo, and two hundred miles away to the northeast is the capital city of Salisbury. The nearest town is Que

Que, to the north, and Selukwe, to the southeast. All the surrounding countryside is sparsely inhabited, somewhat arid scrub known locally as "The Bundu." This, combined with the weather factor, makes it an ideal training ground, where low flying and every other type of exercise could be practiced without too much disturbance to the local population. The air force took great care to stay away from even quite small populations.

Many of the servicemen who served there went back, upon their release from the service, to become settlers in the early postwar years. They were encouraged to do so by the Labour government of Britain at that time and became the backbone of the country along with the families of the early settlers. In October 1951, the Attlee Labour government had become so unpopular that they were forced to go to the country, and a general election had returned Winston Churchill and the Conservatives as the government in power. This was to the great relief of most Rhodesian settlers, as they felt the government in London had estranged them.

In 1951, the problems of Europe seemed far removed from this tranquil part of Africa, but the storm clouds were gathering. The labour force used by the RAF in Rhodesia for guard duties, maintenance of buildings, and other general duties was The King's African Rifle Corps, African troops and NCOs with British officers. Amongst the duties they performed was providing batting service to the RAF officers.

One day, John and three fellow officers found their Batman, or bearer, was absent. John sought out the sergeant major in charge of the bearers, who was a long-serving NCO, of the Matabele tribe, and who had served in the regiment for all his adult life, including the duration of "the war." He was a highly regarded, loyal, and trusted man, and he spoke excellent English. John had got to know him quite well and asked him if he knew what had happened. The sergeant major replied, "Oh! I expect he's gone home for a visit, sir! He's a new recruit, recently from the initial training unit in Kenya. When they come down here and get settled in, they do sometimes just … go."

"Will he come back?" asked John. "Because my dress wristwatch is missing from my bedside table, where I put it last night! Do you think he might have taken it?"

"Yes, sir! That's quite probable, but don't worry, he will come back with it. You see, sir, it's probably been a year since he has seen his family, and he wants to go to them with some token to show them what a fine son they have now, and so trusted that his officer lent him his watch for the journey."

"Well," said John, "didn't he apply for leave and ask for a travel warrant?"

"No, sir, he probably had a message yesterday evening 'on the drums' to say that something was going on in his 'boma,' and he decided to go."

"How will he get there, in that case, and how long will he be gone? Where does he live?"

"He's a Nyasa boy, sir. He'll walk. Probably gone one month, maybe two. Don't worry 'bout your watch, sir. He bring it back, no damage. He'll guard it with his life!"

Two days later, John was scheduled an early-morning solo flight exercise. Shortly after daybreak in the chill morning air, he walked out to the flight line to his assigned Harvard. First he completed his outside aircraft check. Whilst doing this, the ground crew was plugging in the starter battery unit, known as a "Trolley Ack," in preparation for the start-up. The aircraft were parked overnight with both sliding canopies closed. Because it was a solo trip, there would be no one in the rear cockpit, of course, and as John mounted the left wing to gain access to the front cockpit he glanced into the rear cockpit. He noticed, through the closed canopy, that the rear seat straps and canopy were correctly fastened.

Cockpit checks, start-up, and taxi out all followed smoothly, and after an engine run-up, magneto checks and normal checklists were accomplished. With permission from the control tower, John turned onto the active runway with the early morning sun rising behind him; as he faced west, he took off into bright, clear sky. Climbing out from the airfield height of five thousand feet to a safe altitude for a session of aerobatics, he revelled in the wonderfully smooth air at that time of day. As the ground heated in the sun, the conditions grew steadily more turbulent as the day progressed and in the afternoon could become uncomfortably so. Because of this factor, most training flights took place in the morning; afternoons were devoted to ground school and other activities.

Levelling off at ten thousand feet, John began the two clearance turns prior to starting a sequence of aerobatics. As he did so, he noticed a movement down beside his right leg. Looking down, he froze in horror. Slowly rising from the floor was a snake. From the ground school briefings, he recognized it as a black mamba, one of Africa's most dangerous and highly venomous snakes. For a moment he was petrified, and then he began to think of possible options whilst he continued a gentle, steady turn, afraid of making any movement. Looking at the creature, he noticed that it was not in an agitated state. He remembered that, when they were excited, they rear up and extend the neck area behind the head in the same manner as cobras. Furthermore, by nature, when they sense danger, they tend to slide away to the nearest hiding place. They are not as aggressive as the many myths told about them. However comforting that fact may be, it did not help the situation. He continued a turn toward the airfield at Thornhill and gently pressed the "Press to Speak" button on the spade grip, and then softly called Thornhill Tower and reported his position as "five miles to the south of Selukwe at ten thousand feet, climbing, with a snake in the cockpit!"

The controller replied at once, "Are you serious?"

"Affirmative," John replied. After a slight pause, the stock reply of air traffic controllers universally came back. "Stand by!" Then, after a lengthy pause, "Do you want to call an emergency? What are your intentions?"

"I'm heading back toward base and continuing in a steady climb, and, oh yes, I have an emergency!"

"Do you know what type of snake it is, and have you been bitten?"

"I believe it's a black mamba. It hasn't bitten me so far. I'm going to continue climbing, and I hope it will become dormant through lack of oxygen and cold."

"Please keep us advised and steer 155 degrees; we'll keep this channel open for you. Don't bother going to 121.5!"

As he continued to climb, John again took stock of his situation. The cockpit canopy was still open; he would normally have closed it prior to doing any aerobatics, and it was certainly getting very cold with the ever-increasing altitude. Normally, all flying training was done below ten thousand feet, and oxygen was not required. He was, however, wearing an oxygen mask that contained the voice microphone for radio transmissions and a leather flying helmet with the receiver earpieces, and his goggles were down, in place. These items did provide quite good protection for his head, but for the rest of him, all he had was the thin flying overall, thin cape leather gloves, and ordinary socks and shoes. Certainly not "snake proof."

Passing fifteen thousand feet, the tower called again. "Do you know how the snake got there?" John thought, *What a bloody stupid question. Typical!*

Before he could reply, the mellifluous tones of the wing commander flying came over the air. "Hello, Johnny. Sorry about that. How's the situation?"

"Well, sir, I'm going to level off now. I'm at sixteen thousand feet, and it's pointless to try to get any higher. I don't want to get anoxic. The snake seems very docile. It's climbed up my right leg and is about knee level. I'm going to try to get rid of the bloody thing."

"Okay. Do whatever you think best; just keep us advised. Be careful!"

"Roger that, sir!"

At this point, the snake's head slowly turned to the right, away from his leg, and started to lower gently and very sluggishly.

John thought, *It's now or never*, and with a lightning quick movement, released the control column with his right hand, which was about seven or eight inches from the snake's head, and grabbed the snake just behind its head. Simultaneously moving his left hand off the throttle and grabbing hold of the control column, he quickly rolled the Harvard onto its back and then, with all his might, hurled the snake out of the cockpit.

With the aircraft now in an inverted dive, it quickly gathered speed. The front part of the snake was now outside and was being beaten against the side of the aircraft by the slipstream. John realised that it was still attached to something inside. Glancing down, he saw that its tail was wrapped around a part of the seat attachment. Thinking quickly, he changed hands again; controlling the aircraft with his right hand, he used his left hand to slam the cockpit canopy forward, trapping the snake neatly about half way down its body.

At this point, the Harvard was nearing its maximum, never-exceed speed. John rolled upright and, throttling back, gently reduced speed. The front part of the snake, now happily outside, was thrashing about violently in the slipstream. About twelve miles ahead, John, now passing nine thousand feet, could see the airfield ahead. Feeling that he now had the situation under control, he called the tower and reported his status. They came back that they had cleared the field for him, and he was clear to land as he saw fit.

Keeping up the speed at about 150 knots, he saw the snake's body was partially severed, and the bit outside was being beaten against the side of the canopy. A fair bit of blood had smeared back by the slipstream onto the Plexiglas panes behind him. Keeping the speed up, he tore into the circuit pattern, called, "Downwind for landing, full stop." He ran through the landing checklist and turned onto the final approach calling, "Turning finals. Undercarriage down. Three greens," and as an afterthought, "With a snake on board!" Then he brought the aircraft down into a three-point landing.

He turned off the runway followed by a collection of crash crew appliances, including ambulance. Calling "Clear the active runway," he followed with, "I would suggest that the ground crew take great care handling this animal; although it's badly damaged, I think it's still alive and probably very cross!"

He stopped the aircraft on the perimeter track taxiway, shutting down the engine, and two of the fire crew members, clad in all their firefighting gear, approached the snake on the starboard side of the aircraft, one wielding a long pole with a wire noose on the end. The snake was obviously in bad shape, nearly severed in two, and was quite limp. The fireman had no difficulty in securing its neck in the noose. Seeing this accomplished, John slid back the canopy and undid his safety harness, parachute straps, and headset connector. Other ground crewmembers had chocked the wheels and secured the aircraft so, completing the "after shutdown" cockpit checks, he climbed rather shakily out of the cockpit onto the port wing and jumped to the ground, leaving the ground crew to deal with the remains of what proved to be a six foot, six inch black mamba.

The first person to greet him was the wing commander flying, who grabbed him with a warm handshake. "Well done, my boy! Jump in my car, and we'll talk about it on our way." John was still somewhat numb from cold as well as delayed reaction and sat quietly in the Jowett Javelin as they drove along, followed by the ambulance, still trying to comprehend the whole event. "Would you like a cup of coffee?" asked the wing commander conversationally. "What I think I would like is a good stiff drink, sir," replied John. "That's a damned good idea," came the reply. "The MO is following us in the blood wagon; he can't wait to get his hands on you and jab you, of course! Look, what we'll do is slip round to the mess, and I'll get them to open the bar, although it is a bit early. Unusual circumstances and all that! Good excuse anyway, and, to tell you the truth, I think we could all use one! We'll do the debrief there. What a splendid idea!"

Arriving at the mess, closely followed by the ambulance, they trooped into the mess, closely pursued by the medical officer. Having summoned the barman and prevailed upon him to open the bar, the wing commander then ordered large brandies and ginger ale all round.

Word travels quickly under these circumstances, and no sooner had the drinks been served than the station commander entered, closely followed by John's instructor, Flight Lieutenant "Plug" Ramsay. More drinks were ordered and when served, the station commander said, "Jolly well done, Johnny. We were all in the tower and heard what went on. Do you want to tell us all what happened? Oh! Hang on a moment; here's the station flight safety officer just coming through the door. He'll need to hear this too!"

John's flight commander and several other curious souls, eager to hear what they could of the rumours flying around, immediately followed the FSO. More drinks were ordered, including seconds for the early arrivals. At this point the wing commander flying, turning to the station commander, said, "Sir, don't you think it would be a good idea to cancel flying for the rest of the day, so that we can examine all the aircraft to make sure no more are infected?" "Capital idea," replied the station commander, and the company gathered around to hear the firsthand account.

FOUR

Two days after his incident with the snake, John was sitting in the anteroom of the officers' mess having tea and reading a book when he was approached by another officer whom he did not recognise.

"Hello there," said the newcomer. "Do you mind if I sit here with you, I've just arrived from Kumalo this afternoon. My name's Geoff Sanders." He was a mild and inoffensive-looking man, rather older than most of the permanent staff, balding and quite small, rather white faced and a little portly. He had a nondescript face and a pleasant air about him. Johnny introduced himself, and they chatted about generalities, background, hobbies, and sports. Johnny had recently discovered the game of squash. The RAF, in its wisdom, had built a squash court at Thornhill, and it was a well-used facility. "What about a game after tea?" suggested Geoff. "Great!" John replied.

They met on the court and after a warm-up knockabout, the match began. John was very young, very fit, and enthusiastic, and he had automatically adopted the "power game" philosophy. Lots of powerful, aggressive strokes and not too much game planning, strategy or technique. Geoff, in complete contrast, merely moved to the centre of the court and, almost nonchalantly, returned the powerful shots, gently, into the most difficult corners, with the result that he constantly presented John with almost impossible situations. After a brief period, Johnny was exhausted, breathless, and in a lather. Quick to realize that he was completely outclassed, he conceded the match and suggested that after a shower they might retire to the bar for a drink before dinner.

Over a cold Castle Lager, John remarked, "You've played this game before!" Geoff then explained that he had been the South East UK champion some years ago and that he had developed a degree of skill and low animal cunning at the game. He then gently led back to the circumstances of the snake, revealing that he was from the investigative branch at the RAF headquarters at Kumalo and was looking into the case. He revealed that they had discovered a sack under the rear seat in the Harvard, which had been used to carry the mamba. After depositing it, the twine securing the sack had been untied and the canopy closed. A very exhaustive search had been made amongst the ranks of the KAR, who were responsible for guard patrols, and something very important had been discovered. John's bearer's recent absence had been investigated, and it transpired that he had not gone home to his family but, in fact, had travelled all the way north into Kenya, where an underground terrorist movement had begun. The organization had been given the name of Mau Mau and professed to be a "freedom" movement.

"We don't know much about the group at present," said Geoff. "It appears to be the beginning of an uprising. Of course, it's the usual African muddle, and we are trying to find out if it's purely local African or if outsiders are involved. Most of all, however, we are very concerned about the spread of it, and what has happened here gives us great cause for concern. Hopefully this is just an isolated case, but just who took the trouble to move that lad up to Nairobi and return him interests us greatly. He seems to be quite intelligent and has denied meeting with any Europeans."

"That's very interesting," said John. "I have a family friend over here in Bulawayo who runs the brickworks there. He came down from Northern Rhodesia a couple of years ago. I wonder if he's heard anything about it. I'm going to be visiting him in a couple of weeks time whilst I'm on leave. Would you like me to ask him?"

"That might be useful. If he employs a lot of Africans, he may well have heard something. Look, why don't you ask him in confidence? You could begin by saying you've heard a rumour that there's some trouble up north. Have you or any of your lads heard of anything local? If he has, gently get as much info as you can. Okay?"

Two weeks later, John was ensconced on the stoep of Jim Priest's spacious bungalow seven miles to the northeast of Bulawayo, sipping a tall gin and tonic, enjoying the panorama before him, and watching the sunset. After catching up on news of their friends in United Kingdom, Jim remarked to John, "You seem to have become something of name amongst my native workers. There was quite a stir when they heard you were coming here. Far more so than any other visitors we've had." "Oh, why should that be?" John enquired.

"Well I don't really know for sure, but they have given you a name. In Matabele, I'm told it's something like 'The Eagle King Snake Killer.' Whatever you've done, it's made you quite a legend in their eyes. It would seem that you are gifted with magical powers." Then, jokingly, he added, "Can you let me in on the secret? I could certainly use some of that, whatever it might be."

John thought to himself, *What an opportunity*! Then he said, "I wonder if that might have something to do with a little incident that happened a week or so ago." He then went on to recount his episode with the mamba. Jim and his wife, Gwen, listened in awe as the tale unfolded. "Good God! That deserves another drink," said Jim, and he went to fix another round. Whilst he was away, Gwen said, "Jim's right. They really do think you have some unearthly magical powers and are most impressed that you have come here. In fact, they all want to see you and pay you some sort of tribute." She went on, "Look, every weekend they have a big party on Saturday night in their mess hall. They have an old 'umfazi' who spends all week brewing up gallons of mealie beer; you've probably heard of it as 'kaffir' beer. Well, that's it. They all dress up and have quite a feast, followed by a 'booze up' and a dance. It seems they would consider it a great honour if you would grace them with your presence. Would you like to do that?"

"I certainly would," replied John. "It sounds very interesting." Later, after retiring for the night, he thought, *This could be a great opportunity to get information straight from the source and to get a feel for how the African viewed the situation as opposed to the various European opinions.* He fell asleep thinking of the questions he would ask and how to phrase them.

At around 6:00 p.m. on that Saturday, John and his hosts drove over to the compound. The mess hall had been decorated for the occasion, and the band had already started to play. John had been expecting just drums and rattles but was surprised to hear familiar European instruments: a piano, saxophone, violin, and a trumpet. Furthermore, they were quietly playing a slow foxtrot! Entering the mess, they were greeted by the head African foreman of the plant. Jim Priest introduced him to John as 'Charlie.'

Charlie was a small, elegant man with the fine-cut features of the natives of Ethiopia and was immaculately attired in a tuxedo dinner jacket and patent leather shoes to match. He said to Johnny, gravely, in very good English, "Welcome, it's very good to have you here this evening; so many people wanted to see you, and you do us a great honour by coming. We would be honoured if you would accept this small gift from us. It will bring good luck. " He handed John a beautiful, elegant, hand-carved walking stick. John replied, "Thank you, Charlie, I feel honoured that you have asked me here."

The music had faded into silence, and the noise volume in the hall had fallen to a whisper. Every head in the place had turned to look at John and his two friends, Jim and Gwen. Charlie said quietly to John, "I think they would be very pleased if you said a word to them all to break the ice; most of them are a bit frightened to actually see you. They are all quite sure that you are a great spirit in human form."

John paused for a moment then held up his right hand and said to his now silent audience, slowly and clearly, "I am honoured that you people, from so many tribes, have welcomed me to your boma this day. May the good spirits always walk with you!"

There was an instant burst of chatter in various tongues as translations were made; then the expressions of awe turned into smiles, the band began to play again, and the noise volume rose to a normal level. As they walked to the table that had been prepared for them, Jim said quietly to John, "Johnny, that was just right. You couldn't have said anything to please them more. Now I'll have a happy workforce on my hands for a while!" Settling at the table, the three were offered cold iced lager, which Jim and Gwen accepted. John said to Charlie, "I'd really like to try some of what you're drinking." With great ceremony, a foaming pint pot of the milky-coloured beer was placed before John, and again the noise level in the hall fell to a quiet murmur. Taking up the glass, John eyed it, put it to his lips, and drained the whole pint without pause.

Returning the pot gently to the table, he said for all to hear, "That was mushi, mushi!" This utterance caused a great roar of approval, and the volume of music rose again.

As the evening preceded, the food was tasted with great ceremony at their table, and John from time to time asked Charlie a question or two enquiring about his life—where had he came from, how long had he known "Boss Jim," and other mundane generalities. Charlie, under the gentle persuasion of the evening's brew, became quite open with information and mentioned that several of the workers knew of others who were from the northern countries who had been home. There, the talk had been of other foreigners who had paid certain young and educated men to go to Russia for university courses and training. Indeed, some were there now, and one or two had returned already and taken up good jobs in the larger cities. Johnny asked if he thought they had any influence over or were leading the Mau Mau movement. He replied that he had not heard of this, but that it was likely that the locals who had started the movement would be jealous of their position and would resent any interference from these newcomers. The locals would certainly welcome their aid but not as leaders.

After an hour or so, the tempo of the band began to change, and the European style music gave way to the local African "pop" music. Jim indicated to John that this was the time to depart the scene, as more and more booze was flowing, and the tempo was rising. As they drove the short distance to the residence, Jim explained that from this stage on it would get quite tribal, and that the gathering were best left to their own devices, and it was unwise for them to witness or ask questions about the rest of the proceedings.

"Come Monday morning there'll be a queue a mile long at the dispensary, all with massive hangovers and the common complaint of a 'devil in the head' or 'menigi bubble arse.' All we do is to give them a couple of aspirins each for the headache or a dose of jollop to cure the stomach problems. This seems to affect a magical cure, and they all believe it is just that!" explained Jim.

Arriving back at Thornhill, John met with Geoff and imparted all the information he had gleaned. As they were talking, an officer burst into the anteroom and proclaimed, "Have you heard the news? The king has died!"

FIVE

March 20, 1952. RAF Thornhill.

John and his fellow students were formed up in open rank formation, all wearing black armbands on their left arm in mourning for their dead king.

Two days after his death, on the sixth of February, young Princess Elizabeth, who was in Kenya at the time on a visit with Prince Phillip, was proclaimed queen. Thus began the second "Elizabethan Era." Britain, the commonwealth, and all the armed services were in official mourning.

This was the "wings parade," when all of the now-qualified pilots were awarded their wing brevet badges—a very proud and poignant moment for all of them. That evening, their instructors had laid on a big party in the mess, and they could now relax as fellow pilots with their instructors.

One was missing, however. "Plug" Ramsay, John's instructor, had been posted a month before to Eastleigh, outside Nairobi, to fly Harvards with the squadron there on anti "Mau Mau" operations. He had been killed three days earlier during an "op" and had been awarded a posthumous DFC. Amongst the toasts that night, one was for Plug, who had been a wonderful mentor to John.

John had graduated top of the course in flying and had won the aerobatic prize; his academic achievements were, however, rather more modest. Suffice to say, he felt on top of the world. During the course of the celebrations, Geoff Sanders appeared, seemingly from nowhere, and gently eased John away from the main buzz of noisy conversation.

"Congratulations, John. You've done well! Any idea of what you might be doing next?" he asked.

"Well, I've applied for fighter, ground attack role. Don't know if I'll get it, of course. Just have to wait and see."

Geoff looked directly at him and said, "Where would you like to go if you did get it? Middle East? Far East? Second TAF in Germany, perhaps?

After a moment's thought, John replied, "Germany!"

Two days later, John and the others boarded a Central African Airways Vickers Viking, which had landed at Thornhill on charter and then flew them all to Livingstone. Awaiting them there was an Airworks charter Avro York, a wartime-inspired transport development of the Lancaster bomber. Two days later, on a cold, rainy night, they landed at RAF Lyneham, in Wiltshire. Next morning, John awoke to greet the day in a snug little room in the RAF hutted accommodation at Cliffe Pypard used for transit passengers.

It was a cold, clear morning with a sharp hoarfrost, and as the Bedford OB RAF thirty-two-seater bus wound its way down the hill through an avenue of beeches, the sparkling white frost had turn the bucolic landscape into a dreamlike fairyland. John mused to himself that after the dry, parched appearance of Rhodesia, this was paradise, and, what a wonderful place Great Britain was to have as home. The destination was Swindon railway station, where there was a small RAF Rail Transport Office (RTO), which dispensed railway warrants to passengers who arrived by air at Lyneham. Checking in at this office, John found his orders waiting. Go home for two weeks disembarkation leave; then report to RAF Moreton in the Marsh for two weeks of acclimatisation flying, and then it's on to RAF Valley, in Anglesey, for a jet conversion training course.

SIX

April 15, 1952. RAF Moreton in the Marsh.

RAF Moreton in the Marsh was situated just to the east of the delightful Cotswold village of that name. The bucolic countryside was sprinkled with small villages, each with a couple of pubs, hotels, and tearooms. It was so vastly different to the harsh, sere beauty of Rhodesia. To John it seemed like paradise indeed. The RAF was well liked in the area, and young pilots like John were much sought after by the young ladies of the region, another huge difference to the comparative wilderness of Rhodesia. Flying conditions too were so markedly different. In Britain, the constant changes of weather fronts, with all the variations possible, occur with great frequency. Also, situated just to the south of the industrial midlands, industrial haze, mist, fog, and atmospheric pollution were abundant. After the first couple of cross-country flights through these conditions, John remarked that it was like flying around in a bowl of milk!

Navigation, again, was so different. In sparsely inhabited Rhodesia, towns were easily identified, there were few roads, railways, or rivers, and no canals, so when a pilot saw any of these navigational fixes appear on cue, where it should be, there was no ambiguity, and he knew precisely where he was. In Britain, with its countryside patchwork quilt of fields, streams, and rivers—villages, towns, and cities all entwined by an intensively developed network of roads, railways, and canals— navigational confusion abounds, to the bewilderment of the hapless

29

novice aviator. At night, the same degree of confusion exists with a vast profusion of lights everywhere. Moreton in the Marsh had its own little diversion; the main runway happens to be parallel to the main street of the village and is brightly illuminated! Many of the confused young pilots regularly mistook one for the other and, thankfully, were led back to the correct path by a very wary and alert air traffic controller, complete with suitable admonishment.

In conditions of poor visibility and low cloud, instrument flying was a necessity. Britain has an abundance of poor weather, and the pilots had to adapt to these conditions. American aviation had developed a relatively sophisticated radio beacon system of navigation enabling pilots to fly from beacon to beacon along an "airway" and to carry out a primitive instrument approach to landing at the destination—a procedure known as SBA (standard beam approach). From bitter experience during the war, it was found that radio beams could be bent and aircraft misdirected. In addition, the system required a lot of interpretation by the pilot, adding considerably to his workload, and could lead to many pitfalls and hazards in foul weather.

In Britain, the RAF had developed another system. Many operational airfields had RDF (radio direction finders) installed. The only equipment carried in the aircraft was the radio used for communication. A pilot needing directions would call the ground station for a "steer." The ground controller, having identified his transmission, then gave the pilot a course to follow until he was over the airfield at a specified altitude. The pilot was then directed to take up a given heading and start the descent. At a predetermined altitude and distance from the field, the pilot would then be instructed to turn left or right on to an inbound heading toward the runway, descending to a "break-off" altitude below the cloud base, from which point he could make a visual approach and landing. This approach procedure was called a "QGH."

Should the weather be so poor, "below limits" for this procedure, a radar procedure was used, called a "CGA." In this system, the aircraft's position was located by radar and identified by the pilot, giving a signal known as a "squawk" on his IFF (identification friend or foe) set. From that point on, the pilot simply followed the instructions given by the ground controller until the aircraft was about ten miles from the runway. From thence, he handed over to a high definition radar unit and its controller, who proceeded to give a very detailed "talk down" to the runway threshold.

These two systems required very little equipment on the aircraft and no "interpretation" by the pilot, relieving his workload, allowing him to concentrate on flying the aircraft accurately to touchdown in very abysmal weather and visibility. It was remarkably effective but did require expert "talk down" controllers. At Moreton in the Marsh, pilots flew many such approaches and became quite proficient in bad weather flying—a necessary step before moving on to high-speed jet aircraft.

SEVEN

May 15, 1952. RAF Valley, Anglesey, North Wales.

John walked out toward the line of Meteor Mk 7 aircraft with his latest instructor, Flight Lieutenant Bill Edwards, a tall blond Yorkshire man with a great sense of humour. One of the Meteors had the engines running, and for the first time, John experienced the heat of the jet engine's exhaust. It caused the air to shimmer off the concrete parking area and saturated the clean sea air with the redolent smell of burning paraffin oil, known as JP.4, used to fuel the jet engines. All of this seemed to John to herald in a new era, so different from the world of propeller-driven aircraft; it was all incredibly exciting. They approached Meteor tail number WF814 carrying their parachutes over their shoulders. After completing a careful external check of the aircraft, John climbed into the front cockpit of the sleek two-seat machine and strapped in. Bill, the instructor, sat in the rear seat. The heavy canopy, hinged on the right side, was then closed and locked. John took a moment to look around; it was all so different from the Harvard and the Tiger Moth. No engine in front of you, just the windscreen and instrument panel below, the wings set far back; one had to turn one's head to see them.

Bill led John through the engine start procedures and checklists, permission to taxi was obtained, and Bill said, "Off you go then!" Gingerly, John nudged the two throttles forward; apart from a slight increase in noise and engine rpm, nothing much happened. Adding more throttle, the Meteor gently moved forward and gathered speed;

turning the aircraft by applying rudder and a touch of brake, they proceeded around the perimeter track to the active runway. The Meteor rode as smoothly as a luxury car, with far less fuss and noise associated with a propeller-driven aircraft, and was much easier to taxi.

They paused at the entry point to the runway and went through the takeoff brief and checklist; then, cleared for takeoff, John rolled forward and lined up on the centre line. From the rear, Bill said, "Well, go ahead then, take the thing off. You can see a lot more than I can from back here!" "Okay," John replied, "here we go." Opening the throttles to full power, the brakes released, and the Meteor began to accelerate. Slowly at first, and then ever quickening, the constantly increasing push in the back seemingly never ending, quite outside any of his previous flying experience. As the speed approached one hundred knots the aircraft seemed to want to burst free of the ground, and with a gentle back pressure on the control column, the Meteor slipped effortlessly away from the runway and accelerated in a seemingly endless flow of power, far beyond John's expectations. As the undercarriage folded into the retracted position, the Meteor continued to accelerate in a smooth and magical way that felt to be from another dimension. It climbed away, ever faster and so quietly compared with the thrashing, noisy, straining efforts of the piston-engine, propeller-driven aircraft he had been flying until now. This was a completely new, incredible world.

John's jet training moved along its measured lines as smoothly as all his previous training had gone. He quickly adapted to the power lag of engine response and the slow deceleration of the sleek jet aircraft. On May 7, after seven short dual trips in the Meteor, accumulating only three hours forty-five minutes of dual time, he took his first solo flight in the single-seat Vampire Mk 5. The smooth progress was marred by an emergency event whilst on his first low-flying exercise in the Vampire.

One leg of the flight plan took him across Red Wharf Bay on the east coast of Anglesey. Turning onto a northwesterly heading over Puffin Island, heading for Moelfre, John dropped down to fifty feet above the sea and accelerated up to 450 knots. The coastline to his left and ahead was very clear; no sailing boats lay ahead that would be disturbed and aggravated by his high-speed dash across the bay. However, some small dots appeared in his windscreen and grew rapidly in size. In a heartbeat, he was heading directly into a flock of seagulls. At his rapid approach, they began to scatter up, down, and to each side. One, however, remained dead center in the gun sight. Not wanting to hit the large bird with the windshield or canopy, John flicked the control column to the left, and the bird shot past the canopy to the right. At once, he felt a resounding thump on the airframe. Obviously, the seagull had hit some part of the plane. Immediately he throttled back, eased up to two thousand feet, and called RAF Valley to report the problem. Having slowed to two hundred knots, he gingerly tried the controls. The elevator and ailerons seemed unaffected; however, when he tried the rudders, he found they were immovable. Assessing the situation, he realised this would not cause a problem whilst airborne but would affect directional control on landing.

Responding to his call, the approach controller called up an instructor pilot flying another aircraft, and vectored him into formation with John to check on the damage. The report was not good. The bird had struck the aerodynamic "bullet" that covered the joint between the right-hand tail boom and the fin and elevator assembly, peeling the skin of the fin back to the rudder post, wrapping it around the rudder, causing them to jam. John was already heading for the airfield and asked the controller for the prevailing wind speed and direction. As John said later, "Fortune smiles upon the ungodly"—the wind was only blowing five to ten knots and almost straight down the active runway.

The landing went off without incident, having added five knots or so to the normal landing speed. On the runway, as the Vampire slowed, he gave the rudder bar a very hard kick in each direction and appeared to get a little more movement, the rudders now free of any high aerodynamic loads. He applied a touch of brake and was able to keep the Vampire on or near the centreline. As the end of the runway closed, he once again tried the hard kick treatment, without success. As he slowed to a crawl, he tried to apply rudder and brake to turn off the runway onto the perimeter taxiway; however, it was apparent he would not be able to make the full turn but did manage to clear the active runway. Just!

Reporting his dilemma to the ground controller, he found his aircraft surrounded by eager crash crews and equipment. Shutting down the engine and opening the canopy, he smiled benignly at the anxious-looking flight sergeant in charge of the proceedings and politely asked if he could oblige with a tow. A towing bar and tractor were hooked onto the nosewheel and the whole parade of vehicles proceeded to the parking area, where a large audience of spectators awaited their arrival. Once parked, John climbed out of the Vampire and strolled around to join the crowd examining the unholy mess around the tail assembly. There were a number of exclamations of, "You were bloody lucky!" "Well done, old lad!" and, "Just look at that mess!" Indeed, it was. Fifteen pounds, or so, of seagull at a closing speed of 450 knots causes an impressive amount of structural damage to an aluminum-skinned airframe. Someone remarked, "Good grief, look at that. It's even bent the rudder post!" Bill Edwards had joined the throng by this time and immediately asked John, "How do you feel, Johnny? Are you all right?" "Thank you, sir, I'm okay. Feel a damned sight better than the bloody seagull, and that's a fact!"

Later, on that Friday evening, John joined a crowd of friends who had sojourned, by RAF-issue bicycles, across the airfield, then via a track over the sand dunes across a little wooden bridge crossing a small stream, and then into the little village of Rhosneigr. There, in the rear rooms and glass conservatory of a Victorian boardinghouse, lay "Auntie Tatties." An alfresco pub and drinking establishment known to the cognizant and discriminating aircrew members as being the "in" place to go for a good night's boozing with no closing hour. His episode with the seagull and of the damage caused was a good starting point for a party. The trip back to the airfield was hilarious and fraught with hazards, as one after the other fell off or collided with various obstructions along the way. Only two poor souls ended up in the stream. The following morning saw a few of the stalwarts at breakfast in the mess; the less fortunate were nursing monumental hangovers.

A couple of weeks later, in a small office in Adastral House in Whitehall, Geoff Sanders met with his superiors, and the subject of their meeting was John.

"How is your prospect coming along?" he was asked by the group captain of the Intelligence Branch.

"Very well indeed," Geoff replied, and then went on to give a summary of his unknowing prospect's progress.

"He is, as we know, an average sort of young man who is maturing fast. Five foot ten inches tall, quite lean and very fit. Of average build, mousy-coloured light brown hair, blue eyes with a fair complexion. He is not unattractive in appearance and has no remarkable facial features that would make him stand out in a crowd. He is attractive to the opposite sex and seems to be only attracted to good-looking women. He has displayed an aversion to homosexuals. He is a good mixer, well liked by his contemporaries. His instructors have taken quite a shine to him, possibly because of his ability. Suffice to say, they include him in their circle as a somewhat younger equal. He is a fair athlete, plays rugger moderately well, cricket very well, and is an earnest squash player who learns quickly. It seems that when at home, in Leicestershire, he rides with a couple of hunts and is often invited to their weekend 'do's,' therefore is socially quite acceptable. Medically, as you already know, he is A1, with exceptional eyesight, coordination, and reflexes. His flying record speaks for itself, and his jet training is progressing to the point of exceptional. If we don't use him for our project, he has already been singled out to go directly to Little Rissington for training as a flight instructor. A prospect that he does not relish! He is very keen to get onto a ground attack squadron as soon as possible.

"His background positive vetting has shown he is not particularly politically minded per se but is vehemently anti-Socialist. Overall, a quite stable individual from a good background, slightly immature, but has learned to drink sensibly much of the time and, certainly, when required. He is very 'tight-lipped' on matters of security, is a quick learner, and is blessed with a remarkable capacity for retaining visual images, along with a God-given ability to make instant assessments of situations and make correct snap life or death decisions. This ability has been remarked upon throughout his flight training. A good example of that ability showed up during the accident investigation that has just concluded. His ability to avoid a 'head-on' with the seagull at 450 knots was remarkable, but, in that instant of recognition, he noted that the gull seemed to have a black ring around its beak! We asked a local bird expert to examine the remains before it was removed from the damaged aircraft, and he confirmed that it was indeed a ring-billed gull!

"Finally, he has put up a remarkable performance record on escape and evasion exercises. He seems to disappear into the background, and then turns up, on time, at the rendezvous, appearing seemingly from nowhere. On the last one, we had two observers from the SAS regiment, who remarked that it was 'uncanny' and demonstrated a remarkable degree of stealth and 'low animal cunning.' They added that, if we could spare him, they could use him on the staff at Brecon! To summarize, gentlemen, of those on our 'short list,' he is the best of the few. For our needs, he's my choice by far."

After a very brief discussion, the group captain said, "Very well then, it's decided. He shall go to RAF Celle in Second TAF. That is the ideal location, and there is a squadron there that is re-forming—145 Squadron it shall be! We shall not send him to Pembrey for the normal operational conversion course; if he's that good, he can pick up the tactics and gunnery bit on the squadron!"

EIGHT

September 6, 1952. RAF Celle, Germany.

The "Blue Train" slowly stopped at Celle Banhof in the early evening after its all-day journey from the Hook of Holland, where John had boarded it after a night crossing on the ferry from Harwich. The journey across Holland and then Occupied Germany had been a slow and dull one, passing over the rather boring, flat landscape of the north German plain. Greeting him on the platform was an RTO, who directed him to a waiting vehicle to take him on to the airfield on the outskirts of the small country town.

Darkness had fallen by the time the vehicle pulled up in front of the officers mess. With his two suitcases deposited in the entrance hall, John signed in. Another officer introduced himself. "Hello, I'm Mike Barnes. Welcome to 145. I expect you could do with a drink before dinner. We can show you where your room is later. The boss is in the bar, and he'd like to meet you." Off to the right was a stairway descending to the Keller Bar; seated at the bar were three early customers. The older of them was a slim, elegant man with greying hair. Mike introduced John to him. "Sir, this is John Frazer, our new pilot."

"Hello, John. Welcome to 145. What will you have to drink?"

A couple of drinks later, several more officers had joined the group, including the two flight commanders. John learned that the squadron was not yet up to strength and more newcomers were expected in the coming weeks and months. The commander of B flight introduced himself and told John that he would be with him initially to be "shown the ropes," and when it was considered that he was "up to speed" he would be transferred to A flight, which consisted of "operational" pilots. Once the squadron was up to full complement, B flight would then become operational when all its pilots had achieved that status.

John was shown to his room, and after a swift cleanup, changed into a suit and went back to the mess for dinner. Then followed another session at the bar getting to know people, not just his own squadron members, but those of the two other squadrons stationed at Celle, to say nothing of many other officers from the wing. The majority of them were people who had seen wartime service and had either remained in the service or had been "de-mobbed" or put on the "reserve list." Then, as the cold war had become more intense, they were called back to active duty. John noticed that there were only a handful of people there in uniform that were not wearing wartime medal ribbons. He recognized that he could learn much from their great wealth of experience and quietly made up his mind to make as much use of that as he possibly could.

September and October passed in a blur, every day committed to hard tactical training, both the low-level work, including live air to ground gunnery and rocket firing on the nearby Luneberg Heath range, and high-level, fighter defence tactics and air to air gunnery practice using the cine cameras mounted on the gun sight as a training method. This was vitally necessary to oppose the very visible presence of the Russian air force which was running a good many high-level flights parallel to the "buffer zone" that had been established each side of the demarcation line. The memories and experiences of the Berlin Airlift were very fresh still, and the three "air corridors," which allowed access to Berlin for the Allied aircraft, were closely monitored by both sides. A "battle flight" of four Vampires had been instituted. During periods of tension, these aircraft would sit, fully armed, on a readiness pan near the entrance to the active runway, ready to start up and take off at a moment's notice to face any possible threat. Celle sat near the entrance to the central corridor. This situation gave a certain tension to the training role, John recognizing that real action was possible at any given time as the political situation worsened and that these forward squadrons would be our first line of defence.

The training proceeded rapidly, John's mentors noticed his ability, and he quickly passed through each stage of training. At the end of October, he was declared operational and transferred to A flight. Christmas passed and New Year's Day dawned with the hung-over members of 145 gathering themselves together for a squadron move north to the Friesian island of Sylt. This is situated on the Schleswig peninsula of Germany, adjacent to Denmark. Here, at RAF Sylt, were the air-to-air gunnery ranges over the North Sea, where air-to-air firing practice with live ammunition could be safely carried out. Every year, each squadron of Second TAF spent a month here, under the careful eye of the team of instructors, honing its gunnery skills. This event would finally complete the full training programme for John. He had already demonstrated a degree of accuracy in the air-to-ground gunnery, scoring back at Celle, and his instructors monitored his progress very closely. Again, his natural aptitude allowed him to fall in line with the high scorers from the start.

After the first two weeks of the detachment, the weather turned from being mildly miserable to untenable. Flying weather had been intermittent, and now a powerful North Sea gale was forecast. As the hours progressed the conditions worsened, and the storm increased in force to near hurricane strength. Sylt is a low-lying island some seven miles from the mainland and connected to it by a rail causeway. The highest point on the island is only fifty-two metres above sea level. The North Sea was experiencing historically high tides at the same time. This factor combined with the storm surge made the rail crossing to the mainland impossible and damaged the causeway. In Britain and Holland, all the low-lying land around the North Sea was inundated with floods of historic dimension.

With the cessation of flying, the pilots of the various squadrons had devised ways of amusing themselves by the usual gatherings, centered on the mess bar. During one of these sessions, John became aware of the presence of Geoff Sanders. Seemingly, Geoff had arrived by the last train across the causeway and was now stranded until the weather cleared. "Care for a drink?" asked Geoff. "Not really," John replied. "I think I've had quite enough for a lunchtime session. It's good to see you again. What about a game of squash this afternoon? See if I've improved any since Thornhill."

Later they met at the squash court, and during the course of their game, John casually asked, "Would it be rude of me to ask what you are doing up here in this ungodly place at this time of the year?"

"Not at all. In fact, quite the reverse. I'm actually here to see you," said Geoff.

"Oh, dear! Have I done something wrong again?" enquired John.

"Far from it, my dear chap. In fact, quite the reverse. You appear to be doing everything right, and, as a result, I need to talk to you about a special project that's about to take place which involves you, and I want to know if you want to take part in it."

"This sounds interesting," replied John "What's it all about?"

"I can't really tell you here, but when we've finished this game, let's go over to the office I've had set to one side in the admin building okay. Okay?"

Some forty-five minutes later, John was escorted by an MP and ushered into the office, offered a cup of coffee, and made comfortable.

"Well, John, we can talk at length in here without being disturbed or overheard," Geoff began. "What I'm about to tell you is highly secret, and, before I start, I need to remind you of the Official Secrets Act that you have already sworn to. Also to remind you of the very severe penalties that would follow if you disclose any of this information or even talk to anyone at all about it or mention it casually in passing. Do you understand?"

"Yes, I do."

"Good. Then before we go any further, you're going to have to sign this document to that effect. The information you are about to be given falls into the top-secret classification. You have already been positively vetted for this project, and this is to certify that you are fully aware of all the implications of your future actions. Are you clear about this, or do you have any reservations or questions?"

"Well, I am certainly very aware of the secrecy part of it, and of course I shall observe all the requirements, obviously! As to any reservations, I can't say until I know what it's all about, and what is required of me."

"Just so, but we had to clear that hurdle before I can proceed. Right then! Sign it, and we'll move on."

John signed the paper as required, and Geoff began. "As you are well aware, the Cold War is heating up. We have all sorts of information leaks on our side simply because we have an open government and a free press; that's the nature of things in our society. On the other hand, the Russians have a very tightly controlled system in every way; as a result, it's very difficult for us to come by relevant and useful information. We do have agents on the other side of the Iron Curtain, but they are finding it increasingly difficult to get reports back to us. Signals traffic is fast becoming a science and a war of its own, which GCHQ is fighting tooth and nail. The fact that we have had, and do have, Communist deep cover agents—their fellow travellers and sympathizers working on their behalf and against our interests—is pretty common knowledge. So we find we need to rely on direct face-to-face debriefs of our agents as needed. Here lies the problem. Until recently, our assets on the other side of the curtain have been able to get in and out through certain access points in Berlin. Since the Berlin blockade and airlift, these have been pretty well cut off, and security all along the border itself has been tightened. There were other places where we could slip across, by car even, but with the completion of the wire fences and other security measures it's become nearly impossible. As a result, we have had some casualties, and we now have to overcome all of these measures against us. I would add that the Yanks to the south of us are having the same problems."

"Yes, I do see that," said John. "But how do I fit into all of this, and what do you need me to do? How can I help?"

"Okay, John, you know the Tiger Moth on the station flight at Celle?"

"Yes, I have been flying it, just before coming up here, in fact."

"That has been noticed, and naturally you are current on the aircraft as a result." Here Geoff paused for a moment, and then he continued. "We are replacing that Tiger Moth with a Prentice that will be used as the normal communications aircraft. The Tiger Moth will disappear, as far as most people at Celle are concerned. In fact, it stays at Celle, under deep cover, and will be modified for special duties. Now, this is where you fit in. We want you to fly it!"

"Where to?" asked John.

"Over to the other side of the curtain and back from time to time in order to retrieve and deposit agents. You may recall the work of the Special Op's Squadron during the war, using Lysanders to ferry agents in and out of France? Well, this is the same sort of thing. How do you feel about it?

"Well, it's certainly a lot to think about. Naturally, I'd like to know a lot more about it, but I imagine that that will have to wait until we get back to Celle. Am I right? "

"Spot on. All shall be revealed in the fullness of time, as the saying goes. Obviously, I don't need to re-emphasize the need for absolute secrecy about this. When your squadron returns in ten days' time, I shall contact you down there and quietly introduce you to the other players. okay, okay?"

NINE

On the south side of Celle airfield was an area little visited or known by the majority of personnel based there. It consisted of a series of well-covered and protected bunkered revetments, which were used for ammunition and POL stores; alongside them ran a railway line, which brought in these supplies. It was late evening, operations and flying had ceased some three hours earlier, as a plain dark green Volkswagen drove past the heavily fenced and guarded area through a wide double gate. The driver was Geoff Sanders, and his passenger was John. They drove behind a small copse of dense pine trees, some distance further on from the main collection of bunkers, to a bunker that was rather wider than most and was fitted with double sliding, heavily plated, steel doors. This separate area had its own fenced protection and was very well concealed from view on all sides.

"Well, Geoff, whatever you're going to show me seems to be very secure, if nothing else!" remarked John. "I'd no idea this was here." Geoff shrugged and replied, "I certainly hope so. Only a small handful of people know what's in here, and they have the same security restraints as you. None of the flying or base personnel are in that category, with the exception of the station commander and the intelligence officer. The handful of people you're about to meet are not based here permanently, neither do they live on the station; in fact, a couple of them are not even in the air force!"

Stopping outside the doors, they left the car and went to a small personnel door off to one side; as they approached, Geoff produced a small device about half the size of a cigarette packet. Pressing a button on its top, he waited for a small green light to illuminate; a moment or two passed, and then the door silently opened. No lights were visible. They passed through the door, which closed behind them, and then the lights came on in the roomy office they had entered. A small, middle-aged man dressed in plain dark overalls greeted them. "Evening, Geoff. So who's this you have with you? Our driver, 'Airframes,' for the use of, perhaps? Hello, mi' lad," he said, extending his hand, "Just call me Bill. It's good to meet you."

"Bill is our tame boffin," said Geoff, by way of introduction, "and this is John Frazer, answers to the nickname 'Johnny,' hopefully to be our aviator extraordinaire! As you know, we're here to look at the device."

"Has he been briefed at all?" asked Bill.

"No, that's your bailiwick. You and your lads can fill him in on the details."

Leaving the office, they entered the main hall of the building, which was the size of a small aircraft hangar. It was mainly empty except for a couple of workbenches, a few items of machinery and, standing in the centre of the floor, was a Tiger Moth.

John saw at once that it was different in detail to any Tiger Moth he'd ever seen. The most visible difference was the colour. It was all dark grey and had no identifying markings, added to which it wore large balloon tires, and the normal two-bladed wooden propeller had been replaced with a smaller-diameter, three-bladed metal one. Below the engine hung a device that looked like a large streamlined suitcase.

"We call it 'The Bat.' Come on, I'll show you around," said Bill. "First of all, you've flown this little number before. It's the old station flight one that was replaced with the Prentice a while back. We've worked it over since, as you can see. The paint job is a 'bit special.' It's antiradar paint, and the usual canvas has been replaced with one of these new textile materials. Basically, it will absorb most radar emissions; very 'hush hush' and all that! Some bloke at ICI stumbled on it after working for the last twelve years or so on the concept. Apparently it works! 'They' say it will; we hope!

"Next the engine: it's a standard Gipsy Major, except that it's new and has been very carefully built by the maker—'blueprinted,' as they say in the trade. Balanced statically and dynamically, tested and 'run in' on the bench. It's to standard spec' regarding power but should be ultrareliable. It's also been fitted with a Koffman cartridge starter, so you don't have to swing the prop to start it. You will also see the normal prop has been replaced with this three-bladed job. It is a constant speed with variable pitch. The diameter is smaller, and it has a better ground clearance, of course, just in case you try to tip it on its nose! It has been designed to give you a much better climb performance than the regular item, and it is astonishingly quiet. Cruising at about 2,000 rpm is its best speed—lowest noise and gives you about eighty-five to ninety knots, I'm told. That device hung below on the exhaust pipe is a silencer, believe it or not, and its shape is low drag, as you can see, and it is very effective without absorbing much power, only a couple of horsepower, in fact. Neither can you see any exhaust glow from it.

"The engine cowlings are also a bit fatter than normal; they have a padded lining for soundproofing. One other little job is the normal tailskid has been replaced with a special, rather larger one that has a small wheel set into it. That's so that you can taxi on concrete as well as grass, Oh, yes! The main wheel tyres are fitted with low-pressure tyres that are low hysteresis so that you won't bounce too much on takeoff or landing. We've also fitted the new Chipmunk braking system to the main wheels. I'm sure you know how those work! It means you can operate, basically, off any surface safely. We can also fit skis or floats on it if required. Take a look inside the cockpit, and you'll see it's pretty standard with the exception of the seats. They have been upholstered, and you don't wear a parachute! We can adjust your seat how you like. There are a few other bits and bobs, but we can cover those later. Do you want to try it out?"

"You mean right now?" inquired John. "What about air traffic control and all that?"

"Don't concern yourself about that," said Geoff. "There's nothing scheduled for tonight, and the tower is closed. We just want to see how you get on with it."

The lights in the hangar were dimmed as a couple of the men pushed the aircraft toward the doors. Bill, standing by a control box, operated a switch, and the doors began to open, and the lights went out entirely. Outside, the moon had risen on a clear, cool night with a light, broken cloud cover. On the other side of the airfield, the domestic site and the town behind it seemed to be a blaze of light. Once outside, the wheels were chocked, and one of the men came forward with a fire extinguisher for the start-up. Another came up to Johnny and handed him a leather, fleece-lined Irvin flying jacket and a standard leather flying helmet and a pair of white chamois gloves. "You'll find these are your size, sir!" he said. "Thanks a lot," replied John as he donned the gear. "That's very kind of you; I think I'd be emulating a brass monkey without them!"

Climbing into the rear cockpit, he settled into the bucket seat, which fitted him perfectly. Obviously, someone had gone to a great deal of trouble to tailor the whole cockpit to suit him. Mentally he went through the before start checklist, set the fuel cock "On," set the mixture fully rich, cracked the throttle open a tad, and checked that the ignition switches mounted on the outside of the fuselage to the left were in the "Off" position. Leaning his head to the left, he saw the ground crew helper closing the engine cowling. "You're primed and ready to start," said the young man.

"Okay, switches off, throttle set, hands clear, suck in!" John replied. The man moved to the propeller and hand turned it through a couple of revolutions, then stood clear on the left, and gave John the "thumbs-up" signal. "Clear to start." "Prop clear, switches on, clear to start!" echoed John as he pressed the large new button fixed on a bracket above the throttle. With a gentle cough, the engine started. *My God, this is different; they have been busy*, thought John. There had been no loud bang from the cartridge starter; obviously that had been silenced as well. Throttling back to idle, the engine was barely audible, and it's tick over was smoother than anything he'd experienced before. Turning the cockpit lighting rheostat up, he saw the instruments themselves start to glow with a soft green background, quite different from the standard red cockpit lighting used by the RAF. In addition, the normal gyro-heading indicator had been replaced with a very different, larger compass. Checking the oil pressure and engine rpm at idle, all appeared to be in order, and he then checked the control movements visually before waving the wheel chocks away.

Ahead, he could see the double gates to the airfield opening quite clearly as his night vision adjusted to the silvery moonlight. *A "hunter's moon" if ever there was one!* he thought as he gently opened the throttle. On each wingtip there was a man positioned to guide him through the gate. Rolling along on the concrete taxiway, he tried out the braking system. A handbrake lever fitted on the right side of the cockpit by his knee applied the brakes, and differential steering was applied by simply using the rudder pedals. It all seemed to work very well, thought John as he taxied off the concrete and onto the grass. The wind was blowing gently from the west, so he turned right toward the east end of the airfield. Swinging the nose left and right, he found that the rear skid seemed to work as normal, but the whole aircraft had a wonderfully smooth feel to it, and the engine simply purred away, all very different to a normal Tiger Moth.

The south side of the runway had a clear grass area that extended half of its length, more than adequate for the operation of a Tiger Moth. Pausing at the eastern end of this area, he ran through the short takeoff checklist, including the engine run-up and magneto check, then, turning onto the runway heading, he opened the throttle fully. As the engine ran up to max rpm it was uncannily quiet and free from vibration; the aircraft accelerated and was airborne after a very short takeoff roll. John climbed to a thousand feet, levelled off, and throttled back to 2,000 rpm. As advertised, the already strangely quiet engine noise faded away and became less than the noise of the airflow passing over the surfaces of the aircraft and through its rigging. Looking around, John found the features of the terrain below quite easy to distinguish in the pale silver moonlight, and he relaxed in the smooth passage through the cool night air.

Climbing another thousand feet, he levelled out and tried out the stalling characteristics of the aircraft. Checking the full power stall, he found the aircraft was quite controllable down to thirty knots or so before it entered the stall and subsequently recovered quickly with little loss of height. After exploring its full flight envelope, John turned back toward the airfield, flew a relaxed landing pattern, turned onto the runway heading, and landed gently on the grass strip in a three-point landing, noting that the large wheels did not noticeably lead to any increased tendency to bounce any more than the normal wheels.

Finishing the short landing roll, he turned toward the fenced enclosure and taxied in to the awaiting ground crew.

As he shut down the engine, the crew chocked the wheels, and he climbed out of the cockpit and was immediately beset with a multitude of questions about the aircraft, how it handled, did he have any problems with this and that, etc. Quietly and patiently, he answered these in a calm, unflustered way; then Bill remarked, "Sorry about all the questions. You see, it's the first time anyone has flown the thing, and we really are very interested."

"That I can understand. Let me tell you, it's the nicest Tiger Moth I've ever flown. It handles and performs beautifully; you've done a super job putting it all together. Thank you, all, very much indeed. I can't wait to fly it again."

As he finished, Geoff gently eased him to one side. "Well done, old lad. They really have worked very hard on this project, and it does seem to have met all our expectations. If there are any little things you think of at any time, let us know and we'll do all we can to fix it. By the way, the silencing programme seems to work very well; after you took off, what little sound there was faded away into the background noises, and we didn't even hear you until after you had landed and were taxying in. It was just great!"

As they drove back to the mess, Geoff remarked, "Just remember how discreet this all is; not a word to anyone. Nothing in your logbook, of course. You do understand, don't you?"

"Of course I do. None of this has happened! One thing I would like to know though. When can I fly it again?"

"I will let you know. Rest assured it won't be long; we need to get on with the program as quick as we can!"

TEN

The squadron had recently experienced a change of command; the new "boss" was a charismatic person who instilled a feeling of confidence in the young group of pilots that formed the bulk of the flying personnel. During the war, he had been a "night intruder" pilot flying Mosquitoes. This was a highly skilled job and demanded much of the pilots and crews who flew these missions. Low flying at night is a dangerous task at the best of times; trying to locate targets that are heavily defended, however, requires esoteric skills, to say nothing of a great deal of intestinal fortitude. All this spoke highly of the new leader and the respect he commanded.

The squadron had become pretty efficient at the primary task of day fighter, ground attack, and the pilots were highly enthusiastic about their role, worked hard at it, and strove to be better than any other squadron. The boss, however, decided that their night-flying skills were lacking. To remedy this, he instituted a night-flying programme designed to bring their skills at night to complement those of daylight hours. At first, this move was not universally welcomed by those pilots, who thought the whole scheme fraught with danger. The two-seat Vampire T11 had recently arrived on the squadron, and the boss took each pilot up for a night-flying assessment. Then they were sent on a cross-country flight at two thousand feet altitude, during which they had to identify certain turning points and report what they saw. They then progressed to nighttime formation flying, both close formation and tactical. The final stage was low flying, nap of the earth, to and from a given target, and carrying out a mock attack. All of this required great detail in planning the route and avoiding obstacles such as high tension power cables, built up areas, and terrain. This entire unexpected bonus was welcomed by John, who took every advantage of the opportunity. As a result he found that the task of discreet "moonlighting" flights in the hush-hush Tiger Moth became easier, to say nothing of the fact that he began to feel enormous satisfaction out of this very special little aircraft and the task it was built to perform. One night, Geoff had brought along a newcomer, a tall, dark haired, well built squadron leader with a northern Irish brogue, whom he introduced to John as "Paddy" Malloy. "Paddy here will be your control from now on, Johnny, and you won't be seeing much of me. He will keep an eye on you and give you your briefings and debriefings. I know you two will get along well. I would suggest that you leave separately when we leave here tonight, and perhaps you could casually meet tomorrow night in the bar."

The next evening, John went into the bar and found Paddy already there talking to a couple of administrative officers. One of them, Joe, called over to John and said, "Johnny, come over and meet Squadron Leader Malloy. He's visiting from HQ and mentioned your name; seems you have some mutual friends." John shook hands with Paddy, who said, "I think you know some people from Thornhill?" and went on to mention a few names. Using this as an excuse to leave the other two, John replied, "Good Lord, yes. I've got some snapshots of a bunch of us together. Would you like to see them?" They left the bar, and, once in the main hallway, Paddy said, "Good ploy, that. You know, I think it would be better if we chatted for a moment somewhere quiet where we won't be overheard." In John's room, Paddy said quietly, "The first 'op' is on for tomorrow night. Get over to the hangar at about eight in the evening, after dinner. I would suggest you ride over there on your bike. Okay, okay?"

The next evening had a broken layer of cloud through which the three-quarter moon gave a soft white luminescence. *Perfect for tonight's little outing,* thought John as he pedalled along on his heavy, blue issued bicycle. Arriving at the hangar, which had been nicknamed the "Bat Hangar," he was met at the gate by "Ginger," one of the mechanics, "The boss is in the office, and the bird is all set to fly. We've double-checked everything, twice! So you shouldn't have any problems with her." Inside the office, Paddy stood by a large map desk on which lay a very detailed map of the area to the east of Celle and some aerial photographs. The map was marked very clearly with the line of the Iron Curtain and the buffer zone lying to the west of it.

"Evening, Johnny, me boy. Looks like a good night for your outing. Shall we get started on the brief?" He then went on to point out, in great detail, the area that was to be the landing zone and the route to it and from it. Some forty miles directly east of Celle lay the small village of Karritz. From there, a road ran northwest for two miles or so, and then it crossed over a narrow canal. The bridge lay over a bend in the canal where the canal ran straight to the west and turned forty-five degrees to the northeast. From the bridge, one could only see a short, curved stretch of water before the view was obstructed by trees. On the westerly reach of canal and to the north of it lay a long meadow, hedged in by a row of trees on every side. Just to the east of the field, prior to the curve in the canal, the canal divided, with a branch running off to the southeast. On the north side of the field was a farm track leading from the road but well concealed by an avenue of trees.

"This is about a thousand yards long, Johnny, and has been fallow for about two years now. Our asset in the area has lived there all his life and is decidedly 'anti' our opposition, who have deposed him of his property and just about everybody else in the area. So, we know our 'info' is sound. The surface of the field is dry, and you should have no problems landing or taking off. You've been landing and taking off on far worse during the practice flights." He went on to explain in great detail the routing to and from the DZ, explaining that it avoided heavily populated areas and any major power lines. He also pointed out the critical part of the flight path over the border defences.

"Just how alert the guards in the towers are, we don't know. However, from our own experience, they simply won't hear you or see you. Again, from our experience, any patrols out and about will not recognize you as a plane. The moon and sky conditions should allow you to see the canal easily, and, as you have noted, the canal layout and road bridge make a distinctive landmark." He then briefed Johnny on the signals that would be used and his ETA.

The wind was blowing gently from the west at five to ten knots, perfect for the arrival and departure. The ground party would consist of three people, one of whom would be his passenger, and that person had been properly briefed on how to climb in and out of a Tiger Moth. "Their party will be about a third of the way along the field from the east end. They will be by that small group of trees on the canal bank. From that spot, you will have about 750 yards left for takeoff, which should be okay. Your passenger will only have a small case with him, which he will carry on his lap, as it will be chained to his wrist, poor sod! Now! Have you any questions?"

"What sort of radar coverage do our Red Peril gentry have in that area?" asked John.

"Good question. We have done a lot of sniffing in the area from our side of the line, and so far as we can tell they can't even see normal targets below about fifteen hundred feet, so we very much doubt if they'll see you at two hundred!" replied Paddy.

John slipped on a plain issue flying suit and Irvin jacket, carrying his leather issue headset, walked out to the aircraft, and carried out a quick check around, making sure the front cockpit was totally empty with no obstructions for his passenger. He then climbed into the rear cockpit, ran the mental checklist, started the engine, waved the chocks away, and then taxied out of the opening gate onto the airfield. Reaching the takeoff position that had been carefully chosen to avoid being seen by the GSO camp guards in the POL bunkers, he turned west into the wind, gently opened the throttle, and took off. Levelling off at two hundred feet, he throttled back to 2,000 rpm and turned left away from the airfield onto his first easterly heading.

For February, the temperature was fairly mild, and the warmth from the heavily cowled engine provided some degree of heating in the cockpit area. *Quite pleasant,* thought John as he viewed the surrounding area. *A poacher's moon tonight, for sure.* The lights of the town of Celle stood out brightly to the north and glinted off the small ponds and water features, also the railway tracks, making navigation a relatively simple matter. His flight path cross-country was firmly etched in his mind, and the landmarks were mentally ticked off as they were passed. Approaching the buffer zone, he took a glance at his sectioned route map under the one cockpit light for confirmation of his exact position prior to crossing the line. Satisfied, he took up the new heading across the zone. To his north, he could just see the outline of the roof of one of the lookout towers as he passed over the recently erected wire fences. No searchlights came on, to his relief, and the flight progressed without incident. The night air was smooth, even at that low altitude, making the flight a pleasant experience.

One difference became obvious. To the west of the border all the towns and small villages were brightly lit. To the east, the lighting was far sparser. An intangible feeling of depression seemed to pervade the whole area. It reminded John of wartime in England, and he then felt very akin to the airmen who carried out intruder missions over the same countryside a few years before. Passing his last checkpoint, he checked his timing, fortunately spot on. He saw the canal stretching out ahead of him, directly in a straight line to the east. He turned slightly south and paralleled the canal; ahead he could clearly see the junction of the branch leading off to the southwest. As he neared that point, he saw the road and bridge crossing the canal, and to his left he saw the landing area. On his horizon, to the southeast, he could see the lights of Karritz and, checking both ways, to his great relief, could see no road traffic. Turning left onto his approach to land, he passed over the canal and saw the hedge marking the eastern boundary of the field with a few full-grown trees along it; ahead, the field appeared clear. Just then, a small flash of light, a little way down the field on the left, came on and then off, and then on again. That was it, the signal to say "all clear for landing." Throttling back, he descended the final one hundred feet and landed softly onto a surprisingly smooth field, and, using the wheel brakes, stopped in a very short distance. Sitting there at tickover, he kept his left hand on the throttle. With his right hand, he eased the 9 mm Hi-Power automatic out of his leg pocket, checking that the safety catch was still on, as the gun was already loaded with a round in the chamber and cocked for firing. Two of the three people approaching continued, and one stood well back, covering his approach.

A man of slight build, dressed in a dark leather coat and carrying a briefcase in his left hand, walked behind the wing on the left side and came up to John's cockpit. Whether he knew it or not, his approach was covered by John holding the gun steadily on him, ready to fire through the canvas skin of the cockpit. Reaching the immediate side of the aircraft, he handed Johnny a simple teaspoon. This was the definite prearranged recognition signal that all was well. John heaved an inward sigh of relief and motioned for his passenger to board. Climbing onto the wing, John noticed that he kept his feet carefully on the reinforced walking strip and very competently undid the small cockpit door flap, stepped smoothly into the front cockpit, settled down, strapped in, and donned the flying helmet that John had previously, carefully positioned there for him. John spoke over the intercom, "Evening. Are you ready to go?" "Okay, let's get out of here!" came the reply.

John released the brake, put his gun back into his leg pocket, and opened the throttle; as he accelerated away, he acknowledged the smart salute the escort gave him. The Tiger accelerated quite quickly, to John's relief, and they left the ground with plenty of room left to clear the few well-spaced trees at the far end of the field, although, John noted, he could have easily flown between them if required. They quickly reached the two hundred feet cruising altitude, and, on doing so, he eased back on the throttle and leaned off the mixture and propeller for a comfortable cruise. After a few seconds, the engine began to run roughly, with fluctuating rpm and the occasional cough. Immediately John richened the mixture, with no effect. *Bloody hell,* he cursed under his breath, thought for a minute, and then, *check the ignition switches!* Putting his hand outside on the fuselage, he felt the switches and discovered one was in the "off" position. Flipping it back on, the engine smoothed out and settled back into its customary smooth buzz. *Just like a sewing machine,* he thought, and then on the intercom said to his passenger, "It's okay. Nothing to worry about; they do this from time to time." Silently John thought, *I'll bet he caught his damned big sleeve on them as he climbed aboard. Well, that's one for the lads to sort out! Good thing it didn't happen on takeoff!*

As they were crossing the border, the cloud became solid overcast at about two thousand feet but with quite good visibility below. Leaving the buffer zone, John felt a little more relaxed, and he settled down to take good note of the terrain, given the lack of moonlight. Ahead he saw a luminescence on the cloud ceiling and realized this was the glow from the lights of Celle town, making it easy to spot landmarks such as this prior to arriving at them. Approaching the town, he stayed to the south of the railway line that led southeast past the airfield. The glow from the airfield buildings was clear to see although the airfield lighting was not on. With the reflection off the cloud ceiling, he could easily make out the runway and taxiways. Throttling gently back, he turned slightly right onto the runway heading, lining up on his grass landing strip area to the left. They touched down, ran a short distance past the POL enclosure, and trundled up to the gate of the Bat Hangar. After a minute or so, the gate opened, and they taxied through to be greeted by an anxious ground crew. After shutting down, John and his passenger climbed out of the plane. After a very brief "thanks a lot for the lift, old man!" the passenger was whisked away by Paddy to an awaiting car.

"Any problems at all?" enquired Ginger. "Oh yes! There is a snag," John replied and went on to tell of the problem with the ignition switches.

"Would it be possible to move them and mount them inside the cockpit where the passengers can't interfere with them?" "Oh yes, that shouldn't be difficult at all. Damn! We should have thought of that ourselves. Anyway, we'll get straight on it!"

John went over to the office where Paddy was waiting to debrief him, and they quickly covered all the salient points. "I can't tell you how glad we are that it all went well; the powers that be will be over the moon about this. Great! By the way, we didn't even hear you or see you land. We were listening out for you, but that machine is unearthly quiet. The first indication was that the motion detector we've just installed started to buzz. Then we just caught a glimpse off the propellor as you turned in toward the gate. You may have noticed it opened by itself. That's the first time we used it except for a trial run whilst you were gone." John said, "Well, if there's nothing more, and seeing that it is a Friday night, and only just after ten, the bar will still be going strong. So I think I'll slip off and get in there. Can I line one up for you?" "Oh yes indeed! A good pint of Guinness would just fill the bill! I'll be along very shortly after I've wrapped up here. Must keep our lords and masters happy!"

John parked his bicycle outside the accommodation block, ran inside up to his room, quickly changed into civvies, and then walked quietly over to the mess and down into the cellar bar, where a large crowd was enjoying the usual Friday night impromptu celebration. "Where the devil have you been?" asked "Hatter," one of John's great friends. "Oh, just been out roaming around on the airfield, seeing if there were any hares about or anything else worth poaching! Anyway, how about buying me a drink, you miserable devil. I could slaughter a pint!"

ELEVEN

During the following two weeks, John carried out four more missions, each to a different location, taking passengers each way. On one occasion the load was just a cage of homing pigeons, which were very useful for sending messages back from the Eastern-occupied territories. The weather and moon conditions varied greatly, and he found that, with experience and familiarity he could cope with conditions that were far from ideal. One passenger remarked that the aircraft, apart from being almost silent, was very difficult to see on the ground, particularly against a background of trees. One could catch just a glimpse of it silhouetted against the sky, but on its approach to land and after landing it was virtually invisible. This made finding it, in the dark, a problem. Could some small light be used by the pilot after he had come to a standstill to indicate where he was?

After much discussion with John, the team rigged up a small blue light fastened on the end of a slim pole three feet in length, which, in turn, was fastened to the trailing edge of the rudder. It could be flashed on by pressing a button in the cockpit. The idea being that should unfriendly people take a potshot at the light, they would miss the aircraft. This improvisation was used to good effect on all the subsequent flights, and the passenger, having been briefed accordingly, found it to be a very useful aid in finding the nearly invisible aircraft in the poor light conditions.

March 12, 1953. An event took place that heated up the Cold War to a dangerous level. For some time, the RAF had been sending out Lincoln bombers from the Central Gunnery School at RAF Leconfield, near Beverly in Yorkshire, to fly into Germany on defence exercises on a two-weekly basis. The object was twofold. It gave the fighter squadrons of Second TAF in Germany a chance to practice mock attacks both outbound and inbound to the United Kingdom. Similarly, it also gave the gunners aboard the Lincolns practice against fighter attacks. For these exercises, the belt mechanisms were removed from the mid upper turret and rear turret guns. Only cine cameras were used to assess the results. The aircraft were effectively unarmed. This day, as the lead aircraft neared Kassel, well inside the British zone, two MiG-15s appeared from below the aircraft; after visually inspecting the Lincoln, they turned and carried out a series of attacks on it, without opening fire. All this was recorded by the Lincoln's camera gun sights. To ensure the safety of the aircraft, it immediately turned back onto a westerly heading and returned safely to Leconfield.

Two hours behind this Lincoln came the second one, on a legitimate flight into the twenty-mile-wide northern air corridor to Berlin. Possibly the plane strayed a little off course, effectively cutting the corner, but it was attacked without warning by two, MiG-15s. The starboard wing caught fire and began to break up. Parts of the aircraft fell inside the Russian zone, and the remainder fell near Bleckede on the edge of Luneburg heath, fifteen miles southeast of Hamburg, well inside the British zone. Three of the crew had managed to bail out; one of the parachutes failed to open, but both the other airmen had died as a result of their wounds. A number of German eyewitnesses confirmed that the MiGs had carried out the attacks and that one of the fighters had been shooting at the descending parachutists. These reports were later confirmed by medical evidence of the injuries noted on the bodies of the deceased.

Prime Minister Winston Churchill, speaking in the House of Commons, described the incident as "a wanton attack," and a strong note of protest was handed to the Russians. Eventually they expressed regret over the incident and returned the bodies that had fallen on their side, as well as the wreckage, to RAF Celle.

A week later, a British European Airways Viking on a scheduled flight to Berlin was also attacked by MiGs in the corridor. Two weeks later, a United States Air Force B-50 was also attacked but drove off the two MiGs with very accurate cannon fire. From the first instance of these attacks, all fighter aircraft flying anywhere near the buffer zone operated fully armed on a "fire-back" basis until the crisis gradually cooled down some months later.

March 15, 1953. Two days after the "shoot-down," the need arose for John to make a run across the border. At the briefing, Paddy explained that events on the "other side" had become quite sticky. It would seem that some leak had occurred at a deep level in British security services and that many of their assets in occupied Europe had been compromised. Of course, an exhaustive inquiry had occurred two years earlier, in 1951, when the two British agents, Don McLean and Guy Burgess, had defected to the Russians. They were part of the "Cambridge Group" of agents who had been recruited from Cambridge University (and other intellectual sources) during the late '30s, when the events leading up to the Second World War had been developing. Although strongly anti-Fascist, the academia then, as now, possessed an equally strong Socialist leaning and was very sympathetic to the Russian Communist Party. They also had a very strong "Fellow Traveller" following in the ranks of the Labour Party and British trade unions, the majority of whose shop stewards and leaders were card-carrying members of the British Communist Party.

Many of these people had been active in government during the war, always promoting the interests of the Russians as so-called "allies." Even during the war, trade union members had been calling strikes in British industry to try to force the Allies into a premature "second front" in Europe, which would have been suicidal at the time. Of course, had this action ever been precipitated prematurely, it would have ended in disaster for the Allies and weakened them to a fatal degree. All this would then have suited Stalin's greater strategic plan, which was to so weaken Europe as a whole, allowing his armies to sweep in completely and enslave the whole continent.

Obviously, Paddy went on to say, the leaks had started again in a very serious way, and all was at risk. "Tonight's run might be compromised, but it is vitally important. There is an agent of ours who has been betrayed and is 'on the run.' This whole mission has been cobbled together in haste, so things could be difficult. For God's sake, make doubly sure the recognition signals are exactly right before you land. Okay?"

Approaching the landing field from the last landmark, John dropped down to just above treetop level. From the stratus cloud cover at about fifteen hundred feet a few raindrops had begun to spatter the windscreen. Seeing the field on his left, he turned into wind and made his approach. Then he saw the recognition signal—four quick blips of light. Slipping just over the trees, he throttled back and touched down as soon as possible. The landing run was remarkably short, but, even though smooth, the field had obviously recently been cultivated and planted and was quite soft. He came to an abbreviated stop and gave the blue identification light one quick flash. As he sat there with the engine at tickover, a little farther ahead, on the left, he made out just one figure running toward the plane. Limping slightly, the person ran to his cockpit side and put both hands on his cockpit door flap. Covering the figure from inside with his gun as usual, John leaned his head and gave the challenge words, "Et tu, Brutus?" The reply came back in a feminine voice. "Beware the ides of March!" "Okay," said John. "Hop in."

As she climbed up onto the wing and into the front cockpit, John detected a slight whiff of perfume, which struck a chord; it was Chanel No. 5, very hard to come by at that time, and certainly not available in the east. As she was sitting down, a bright light came on farther up the field on the right-hand side. The beam was waving about, and from its glare, John could see several figures around it. *Oops*, John thought, *looks as if we have some unwanted company*, and he opened up to full throttle and began the take-off run. As the aircraft accelerated and neared the intruders, the beam of light caught his aircraft squarely; still accelerating, he swept past them. As he did so, he saw flashes of light coming from them and felt a rattle of something striking some part of the Tiger Moth. Pulling the aircraft off the ground and clambering away at a low airspeed, he felt something hit the back of his seat with a very hard bang and a thump in his lower back. Staying low, he slipped over some trees and turned onto his first return course.

The weather had worsened, with the rain increasing as he flew west. Approaching the border zone, he heard the sound of a jet aircraft passing overhead in the clouds. It passed away; then, a short time later, it came overhead again. The crossing point lay just ahead and John pondered, *I wonder if they have some inkling about this route? Could be they have me quartered. In which case I'd better not fly into a trap!* Promptly, he turned ninety degrees to the right and flew for about four minutes on that heading before turning back onto the original heading. As he crossed over the line, a blaze of lights lit up the low cloud some way to his left, accompanied by a great deal of what appeared to be flashes from small-arms fire, plus some heavier tracer ordnance. As he passed out of the zone, the flashes faded away, and he breathed a momentary sigh of relief. The weather, however, was worsening, as was the visibility. He maintained his heading, making a mental adjustment for the alteration of course. *This should bring me over the town*, he thought, and settled in to concentrate on picking up some distinctive landmark.

"How are you doing in the front?" he enquired over the intercom.

"Okay, thanks," came the reply.

"It got a bit hectic back there. Sorry about that! Are you hurt at all?"

"I'm okay; just a bit scared. Do you know where we are?" the passenger asked with a hint of nervousness.

"Well, by my reckoning we should reach our airfield in about twenty-five minutes."

After some fifteen minutes had passed, a glow appeared through the mist ahead, which increased as they drew closer. On his right, he saw the railway line from the north glinting quite well in the gloom. Turning to follow it, he began to notice various landmarks that told him this was Celle. Then he saw the branch line off toward the airfield. Following that, he crossed the path of the main runway and turned slightly right to land on the grass field. As they taxied toward the Bat Hangar, he said to his passenger, "Well here we are, safe and hopefully sound. Are you okay?"

"Not too bad, but I do need to go to the bathroom," came the reply. Shutting down the aircraft, John got out of the seat and stood on the wing to help his passenger out of the cockpit. They climbed down to the ground to be met by an anxious Paddy. "Everything all right?' he inquired.

"The lady needs the bathroom urgently, and then I think she may need some medical attention."

"Well, I have got a doctor waiting inside. I had a feeling you might need one, so I brought him along just in case."

Two days later, John was in the mess having afternoon tea and reading a magazine when he was joined by Paddy, who took an adjacent easy chair. After a nonchalant greeting, twenty minutes or so later, Paddy murmured in order not to be overheard in the low buzz of conversation, "Can you spare a moment? Perhaps in your room? You leave first." John nodded slightly in assent. After five minutes or so had elapsed, he got up, strolled over to the magazine table and replaced the one he had been reading, ambled out of the anteroom, left the mess, and strolled over to his room in the accomodation block. Ten minutes or so elapsed before there was a knock on his door. "Come in," he said, and Paddy entered.

"Good bit of work the other day," Paddy started. "Our masters were graciously pleased with our efforts, and it would seem that you have impressed them greatly with your retrieval of the asset."

"Thank God I've done something right for once!" was the quick reply.

"Well, it would seem so, but I need to bring you up-to-date on the situation. This is the way things stand. Since the shoot-down, things have gone from bad to worse. It's become very apparent that there is a direct leak to Moscow from our side. We know it isn't at this end but from much higher up the line. Just where remains to be seen."

"Point is," he went on, "the young lady you brought across the other night was a very important link. She is the daughter of a German industrialist who has been on our side since well before the war. During the Nazi regime, he was very useful to our side. His family has land and holdings in East Germany, so, of course, when the Ruskis moved in in '45, he lost the lot on that side. Naturally, he still has many connections, and his daughter was over there ostensibly tending to a sick aunt. During her stay there, she has acted as a conduit for our agents and has been invaluable to us. Overnight her cover was blown, and we had to extract her. Thank God, we managed to. It's obvious that they knew exactly where you would be picking her up, and her getaway was hectic, to say the least, as you no doubt noticed! She sprained her ankle as she was leaving the car, and it was sheer guts and adrenaline that she made it to the aircraft. It seems her driver was about to be captured, but he started shooting and was gunned down and killed instantly, we now know. You may also be interested to know the object that struck your seat and gave you a sore back was a 7.62 millimetre round from the Russians' Avtomat Kalashnikov 47 assault rifle. You were very lucky; the round came from about ninety degrees from your right, as you passed the opposition. One had gone straight through the fuselage just in front of you, and this one behind. I would add that you collected twenty-three hits on the aircraft altogether, both 9 millimetre and 7.62. Your passenger did get a burn from one of them; it grazed her right forearm. You can thank your lucky stars you touched down and stopped early. They were much farther up the field, and you just got away with it by the skin of your teeth! By the way, the young lady in question is quite safe and recovering well; she thanks you for saving her life. God knows, had the buggers caught her they would have taken her apart bit by bit."

"We were damned lucky then, it would seem. I'm glad she's okay. Is the aircraft all right?" inquired John.

"Yes, fortunately nothing important was hit. None of the control cables to the tail. Really, there were just the holes in the canvas, and they found a couple of stray rounds that had hit metal parts and came to rest inside."

"Well, where does that leave us, and what lies ahead?" asked John.

"For the moment, nothing. We just have to wait and see. Obviously, there's an investigation going on to try to find the leak. God knows what that will find; my feeling is that we shan't be doing anything soon, so you can sit back and relax until further notice."

TWELVE

The squadron had been busy in the meantime with practice formation flights for a flypast in honour of a royal visitor. HRH the Duke of Edinburgh was to visit Celle on the nineteenth of March during his visit to Second TAF. The security measures for this event had been a good cover for Paddy's presence. The visit went off smoothly on the day, and the visit was a great success. In the mess that evening an impromptu party evolved, during which Paddy drew John to one side and indicated they needed to talk. A little later, Johnny slipped back to his room; Paddy followed some twenty minutes later. Paddy began, "We have been stood down, for the duration, because of the security problem. However, a new program is emerging, and you are to be part of it. I shall be briefing you on it at the appropriate time and place. okay, okay? Johnny acknowledged, and Paddy left the room; John returned to the party. The rest of the month passed without incident, to the relief of all, and life resumed its normal pace.

May 14, 1953.

The boss called John into his office, sat him down, and said, "Johnny, it seems that you are in demand. Command wants you to go up to Sylt for a gunnery conference, and they need you there for tomorrow morning. I've arranged for you to fly up there in the Meteor VII this afternoon. You'll take PO Ross with you; he'll give you your annual instrument check on the way and then bring the aircraft back. When the conference is over, you can bring back a Vampire, which has been up there undergoing repairs. Okay?"

"Yes, sir," John replied. "How long will the conference be?"

"That I don't know; I guess as long as it takes, maybe a few days. You'd better take a change of clothes and some 'civvies' with you; from my experience of these affairs, you may well need them!"

Late afternoon, John checked into the mess at Sylt and went to the room he had been allocated. Entering, much to his surprise, he found Paddy. "Good to see you," Paddy said. "I believe you'll be here for a couple of days waiting for your aircraft?"

"Right, a bit of a swan, I suppose. It's good to see you, though."

"Well, whilst you're here there is something else we need you to do for us. Tomorrow morning I want you to go to the Hotel Miramar in town; sit outside at the rear of the place on the terrace overlooking the beach. Be there by about ten o'clock. You'll be meeting someone there, who will know what you look like, but you won't know him. He is a German, so don't be surprised. He's a very good man and is involved with us. Do answer any questions he may ask; simply be straightforward with him. You can trust him implicitly, I can assure you. Oh yes! I want you to wear civvies; sports jacket and flannels will be fine. You'll find a Land Rover parked outside the mess with the keys in it. Use that. Okay! Now, any questions?"

Later, in the bar, John met up with some of his friends who were gunnery instructors on the staff there and discovered that the meeting for the following day had been cancelled, also that his Vampire would be ready to go in the afternoon.

Next morning, John took the Land Rover he had been allocated for his stay and drove into town wearing his civilian clothes, parked outside the hotel, and wandered through, out onto the terrace overlooking the beach, and sat at a table where he could observe the whole area. A waiter came to him, and John ordered a coffee and took up the book he had brought with him and started to read. The coffee was served, and some ten minutes or so later, at exactly ten o'clock, a man of about fifty-five to sixty years of age came from the hotel and over to John's table. "May I sit with you?" he asked. John stood and said, "How do you do. I'm John Ferguson," and extended his hand in greeting. The stranger returned his handshake with a firm, warm grip and then said, "My name is not important. Perhaps you might call me 'Herr Schmidt' for convention's sake, or perhaps 'Hans' informally?"

"Please do have a seat. Can I get you a cup of coffee, or something stronger?" John inquired.

"Thank you; there is coffee coming for us both."

They sat, and Hans said, "I have been anxious to meet you. I owe you a great deal."

"Oh, why is that?" John enquired.

"Well another is involved; perhaps I should introduce her." Turning toward the hotel he indicated, and from the French doors emerged a very lovely young lady; she approached their table.

"Allow me to introduce my daughter, sir. This is Michelle; Michelle, this is the gallant flying officer you flew with recently, John Ferguson."

"Michelle, how do you do?" John replied formally, taking her hand in greeting. "I hope your trip was not too uncomfortable, despite the weather?"

She lightly squeezed his hand and replied in very good English, "Far from it; from what I remember it was a very smooth flight despite a hectic getaway!" John smiled and then asked, "I hope you've recovered. I know you were wounded?'

"Oh yes, there's just a scar left, not too noticeable. My ankle is just about back to normal now, but I have you to thank, so very much; you did save my life. I'm so glad that I'm able thank you personally."

"Oh, any time. It's a pleasure; glad we could be of service." Johnny stumbled for words. Her father then said, "Should you ever be in the Cologne area, perhaps we could meet, and we could entertain you at home?" and handed Johnny a visiting card with an address and telephone number on it.

"That would be splendid. Thank you," said John. "If I'm in that area I certainly shall. It's very kind of you. Look I'm so sorry to cut this short, but I do have to get back to the airfield; my plane will be ready to go, and I'm expected back at Celle. This really is most kind of you to take so much trouble. I really do look forward to meeting you again."

With that he took his leave and drove back to the airfield. As he flew back to Celle, he pondered over the meeting, savouring the memory of the beautiful young woman and silently vowing to make sure he did get to Cologne to take up the invitation, and soon, if at all possible. How did all this fit together? There must be much more to it. *Yes, I'll grill Paddy about it when I see him, the old devil,* he mused to himself.

A few days later, he was in the mess bar when in walked Paddy. John bought him a drink and asked if they could meet soon to go over the events that had taken place. "It was a very cleverly contrived coincidence," John remarked, "but a very pleasant one, I must say. Thanks a lot!"

"Not at all. Thought you might just enjoy it. I heard they were up there while she recuperated." Next morning they met in an office that Paddy used when he was at Celle, and John debriefed him on the event. Paddy remarked, "You should be able to take them up on the invite fairly soon! A couple of months from now, some improvements are going to be made to the runway here. Your squadron is going to be deployed to Butzwielerhof, on the outskirts of Cologne, for that period. Keep it under your hat until you hear about it officially. Okay?"

"Yes, of course. I shall look forward to that, but what about the 'no fraternization' order?" inquired John.

"Well, it so happens that with the normalization of relations happening next year, we shall no longer be the occupying powers, but simply a part of NATO. The word is that we are now making friendly overtures to the local gentry, so the 'no frat' order has been quietly rescinded. In fact, your little act has been unofficially heralded by all concerned as a firm step toward cementing good relations, so enjoy it while you can!"

THIRTEEN

RAF Butzweilerhof, an airfield situated on the west side of Cologne, was used primarily by the Royal Air Force's Airfield Construction Branch. It had three runways of differing surfaces—one normal concrete, one of the ubiquitous perforated steel pavement strips (PSP), and a unique one of rolled earth covered with tarred paper, similar to roofing felt. The latter was not to be used by the Vampires due to the fact that their low-slung jet-exhaust pipes tended to either set the tarred paper on fire and/or blow the paper away. Also, in wet and slippery conditions, it made an ideal skidpan. Not very good for braking a jet aircraft on its landing run! The squadron did not use the latter. One other problem was that a local German civilian gliding club also used the airfield at weekends. The fact that high-performance jets were now based there for a period attracted a great deal of interest and curiosity to the citizens of Cologne and its surrounding area. For the first two weekends, huge crowds of people gathered to gawk at the jet aircraft, and they constituted quite a security problem.

The squadron flew in on a Friday afternoon. After parking the aircraft and after settling into the operations centre, the aircrew climbed into a bus and was driven round to the officers mess. As they approached, they saw an immaculate prewar Mercedes 540SK white drophead coupe parked outside. In it sat the driver, a stunningly beautiful young brunette. This apparition drew a great deal of favourable comment from the admiring pilots. As they were leaving the bus, she waved at them, got out of the car, and approached; then, seeing John, she ran to him and embraced him. For a moment they paused, looking at each other, then she kissed him lightly on the lips and led him to her car. They sat for a while simply looking at each other, and then John said, "Michelle, that's probably the nicest surprise greeting I've ever had."

She smiled and replied, "We'd heard you were flying in today so I thought I would come and see you arrive. It's so good to see you again. Are you well? Since we met so briefly at Sylt, I've wanted to see you again."

"Look," said John, "I really need to go and settle into my room and sort myself out now, but can we get together early this evening?"

"Of course. We were hoping you would be able to come to our home this evening and have dinner with us. Father wants to see you again, and my mother is so full of curiosity she can hardly restrain herself! Look, I have some shopping I need to do in town. Perhaps I could pick you up at, say six? Then we could be there for sevenish."

"Perfect. I'll be ready and waiting when you get here," said John.

"You'd best bring an overnight kit; you have been invited for the evening, and we do live a fair way from the city."

Walking into the mess, he was met with a barrage of questions from his envious companions, to whom he casually announced, "The lady's family are friends of mine."

"Lucky so and so!" remarked Hatter. "Does she have a sister?"

"Yes, she does, as a matter of fact. Her little sister is just six years old. I think that's a bit too young, even for you, Hatter!" With that, John signed in and quickly departed to his room. At five minutes to six, he walked to the entrance hall of the mess just as the car drew up outside. Walking out, he opened the passenger door, put his small case in the rear seat, slid into the passenger seat, and they drove away.

They drove out onto the Militar Ring Strasse and then took the right turn onto the main road for Duren. She drove smoothly, quickly, and professionally with no wasted time or exaggerated manoeuvres. The large touring car responded to her touch, and although the controls were heavy to operate, she wasted no effort in handling it. John noticed that she was relaxed the whole time but concentrated on driving without needless chatter. Feeling very much at ease with her expert touch, he relaxed and took notice of their whereabouts and the countryside.

Duren is about thirty-two kilometres to the west of Cologne, and from there, they turned south toward Euskirchen, and then, shortly after, turned right onto a secondary road to Nidegen and Monschau. Shortly they left that road, turning left into a fairly well concealed, unmarked but well paved narrow road that wound through the undulating terrain. Then, rounding a bend, the wooded countryside opened up into well-kept parkland running down to a large lake. Rounding another bend, the road led up a hill to a large and elegant house overlooking the lake. It was imposing but not ostentatious, and it exuded good taste.

Drawing up to the front entrance, they were met by a servant, who greeted them and took John's case from him. Another appeared and drove the car away. As they entered, Michelle's father and mother greeted them. She was a slim and elegant lady, who welcomed John with a perfect English accent; Hans introduced her as Elizabeth and then led the way into a pleasant reception room off the main hallway. From the full-length windows, there was a splendid view of the lake in the setting sun. Set in one corner was a very adequate bar, on which stood a cooler of champagne and a tray of glasses.

"A drink, perhaps, for the weary travellers?" enquired Hans. "I do hope Michelle didn't scare you with her reckless driving!"

"Far from it," John replied. "She drives superbly. Whoever taught her did a magnificent job."

"Thank you," said Elizabeth. "I think she turned out quite well."

Hans broke in, saying, "John, Elizabeth taught her to drive when she was fourteen, and I would add that Elizabeth's father was a well-known British racing driver you may have heard of." He then mentioned a very successful person, renowned in motor racing circles, as he poured out four flutes of crystal.

A little while later, over dinner, they spoke of each other's backgrounds. John was intrigued to hear that Hans was from a prominent family of German industrialists that possessed extensive estates throughout Europe. His mother was from Buckingham and had met Hans's father in Switzerland, where she had attended finishing school. They had literally met on the ski slopes. Hans, in due course, attended Oxford for his master's degree and whilst there had met Elizabeth, whose home was in Leicestershire. During the rise to power of Hitler and the Nazi regime, they found themselves in an untenable position. They resolved this by taking residence in Switzerland, where the family had a home, and made this their headquarters for the industrial concerns. During the course of hostilities, Hans and Elizabeth had worked closely with the British and American entities. They were very active in smuggling Allied airmen past the Swiss authorities and into the underground network to return them to England. After D-day, Hans had slipped into France and had worked closely with the Allies, acting as a conduit and liaison between disillusioned members of Admiral Canaris's Abwher.

The admiral and Hans's father had been close friends and the admiral's distaste, and latterly ill-disguised disgust, with the Nazi Party was known to a discreet circle of international figures. Canaris had supported Hitler in the early days, primarily because he seemed to be the only option against Communism; he had never been a member of the Nazi Party. In fact, he had rapidly become disenchanted with the behaviour of the organization well before World War II and had already set up a very clandestine contact with the British Secret Service. Later he had actively been involved with the group of loyal German officers that sought to assassinate Hitler. In an attempt to end hostilities, he had passed vital information to the British via his contacts in Spain and Switzerland, of which Hans had been a very active member. This information was not widely known. Ultimately, just before the total defeat of the Nazis, Canaris had been unmasked by Himmler and executed on April 9, 1945.

All these people were sworn enemies of Communism and dedicated to the defeat of the USSR and its tentacles that were spreading across the world. As the Allied armies had occupied western Germany, many of these patriots had come forward and had been verified by the people who had been working with the Allied intelligence forces. They were then used to establish relations with the populace as a whole; then, in conjunction with the occupying powers, they set up a basic civil control organization working under the guidance of the Allied Control Commission. Hans and others, working with the intelligence organizations, had become instrumental in not only rooting out old Nazi factions that had gone underground but also the cells of Communists that had become extremely active all over Western Europe.

In the early postwar period, relatives of families in eastern Germany, who lived in the west, were allowed by the Russians to visit their families in the east. However, those in the east were not allowed to travel to the west. This situation had caused many problems for families such as Hans's, who had property there (which had been confiscated by the East German Communist government) and also family relatives. The fact that Hans and others were able to drive over the border to visit led to some very ingenious methods of smuggling individuals and items to and fro. In those days, only the main roads had checkpoints, but there were many unpaved farm roads and logging access trails in the heavily forested areas that were usable. These had become avenues of opportunity for such activities, and an ever-growing situation had evolved between the opposing sides of ambushes and clashes.

As the evening proceeded, John learned that Michelle and some of her young friends had become involved in these proceedings, as drivers. The hectic cross-country chases that took place had resulted in many of the operators being caught in the web, with unpleasant results ensuing. Those that had not been caught were the most able and best-prepared ones. Such expeditions required immaculate intelligence, planning, and execution. It spoke highly of Michelle's abilities and support structure that she had not been caught, although she had had some very narrow escapes. The completion of the physical "wall" itself had put an end to such capers, and limited access was now only possible through a few very tightly controlled crossing points.

It was imperative that certain key people had to be moved across the border, and this is why the aerial transport method, using the clandestine Tiger Moth, had been initiated. Michelle had been stuck on the other side when the noose had been tightened. During that time, she had been passed some very vital information about military matters and some important developments that were to take place. The names of certain individuals involved were also part of this highly sensitive intelligence. Accordingly, she had needed to get back to the West to ensure this information was delivered safely to only a few trusted people.

Dinner over, they retired to the drawing room and spent an hour or so chatting about John's family and his pursuits at home in England. Elizabeth was very curious and became quite animated when John spoke of his hunting activities. It seemed that she knew one or two of the people John mentioned, and as the evening passed, the atmosphere became very relaxed.

Later, Michelle said to John, "It's a beautiful evening, and there's a full moon. The lake always looks so lovely when it's like this. Would you care to take a stroll with me and see it?"

"That would be marvellous!" exclaimed John, almost too enthusiastically.

As they strolled in the moonlight toward a gazebo on the lakeshore, Michelle put her arm through his and talked of her friends and their activities. They sat for a while enjoying the warm evening and beautiful view. "Sometimes I wish it could stay like this forever," she said. "It's always so lovely here, but there always seems so much trouble everywhere else, and we seem so involved with it."

John turned his head toward her and looked at her. "But not at this moment, thank heavens. We both know tomorrow is another day, but, sincerely, I shall not forget this one in a hurry." She leaned toward him, looking into his eyes for a long moment, and he gently kissed her.

They sat talking for a short while before walking back to the house. Inside they paused for a moment at the top of the staircase; Michelle kissed John softly and said, "I have enjoyed this evening, so very much. It seems I've known you for a lifetime."

"We shall meet again," replied John. "I do hope that won't be too distant future. Perhaps you could come into Cologne one evening, and we could have dinner together?"

The next day, Michelle drove him back to Butzweilerhof, and after they said farewell, John paused for a moment, watching the Mercedes drive away; he turned and walked into the mess with many thoughts and emotions racing through his mind. Sundays tended to be somewhat torpid days in fighter station messes. The preponderance of pilots was generally late arising, sleeping off the effects of the two previous nights of partying. After depositing his overnight bag in his room, John wandered back to the anteroom to read a magazine or two before lunch. The room was almost empty of people; all there were preoccupied with newspapers and other reading matter. Almost unnoticed, in a quiet corner, sat Paddy, who quietly nodded to John, who went over to greet him. "Care for a stroll?" he asked John. "Well, it's a very pleasant morning. That would be very nice," he replied.

As they strolled around the airfield in the clear morning air, Paddy enquired about his visit and overnight stay and what were his impressions. John described the whole event and expressed his pleasure about the visit. Paddy then gently probed him about his feelings toward Michelle.

"Well, she's a lovely person," John emoted. "I am very attracted to her. I suppose that natural. Who wouldn't be? Am I falling in love with her? That's another question, and one I'm not sure about. It's too early to tell. The way I feel at present is that I really don't want to become too involved with anyone. After all, I'm hardly in what one might call 'a safe profession'; anything could happen to me, and I don't think that would be fair to any lady."

"Sad to say, I'm glad that's the way you feel about it," said Paddy. "It's best if we can stay clear of deep feelings about people we work with. So often we have to 'use them' in a way that would be unconscionable to one who we dearly love. In any case, there are things in the pipeline that involve you and your future that need you to be clear of any deep relationships."

"Oh, what may they be?" John asked.

"Well several things are coming up in the near future. The main one is trying to find this 'leak' we have in our security. In the meantime, however, and of more concern to you, is a course you will be attending later this year."

"Really, which one it is that?"

"Well, your boss will be telling you that you have been scheduled to go on the gunnery instructors course at RAF Leconfield. We see that you are due for quite a bit of leave. Now! Let me suggest that prior to going on the course, you take some leave."

"Well, I don't know that I really feel a pressing need to go on leave right now," John interjected.

"Well, how can I put this? We want you to go on a specialist course that isn't on the list of 'official' courses. If you 'take leave,' it covers a multitude of sins, errors, and omissions, if you follow me. It lasts about two weeks and is one we very much want you to attend. After it, you could take a few days or so, visiting family or friends, and then go on to Leconfield."

"Okay, whatever our masters need! I must say it all sounds very interesting."

"All right then; just carry on with normal duties. When you get back to Celle, there may be some more 'moonlighting' in the offing. There have been a few modifications, and we'd certainly like you to look those over and see if you approve."

A week later, John was called to the Bat Hangar by Paddy. The Moth was surrounded by the team, working away at various items. Bill saw them and said, "Just the man we need. Come over here, Johnny, take a look at this and tell me what you think." He went on to explain the modifications. "My friends at Chobham have come up with this very lightweight armor protection. It's a layered composite material that will stop most ordinances under .45; it's been fitted to the sides of each cockpit and underneath. Yes, we have left a small area clear on each side of your seat so that you can fire your sidearm through! Also, the top and bottom of the fuel tank have been protected along with the fuel pipe down to the engine. You will notice the engine covers have been redone. The new armor forms the outside cowling, and the insulation is also improved. The whole thing is even quieter than before."

"But how much heavier is it?" asked John.

"That's the trick! It's actually only twenty-two pounds heavier but a hell of a lot safer. You'll also see the paint is now grey and black, which gives a better camouflage effect. Lastly, the great trick of all! Total silence, or very near, anyway. As you know, Johnny, even though the engine is remarkably quiet, you could still hear a whistle from the rigging wires and various bits of the airframe. Well, the friends have been working on this problem for other projects, and they've come up with this. It's an electronic device that is tuned to various sound frequencies. It then produces another sound frequency that opposes the first and cancels it out. It's still early days with it, but it's basically very simple and weighs very little. There's a sensor, a vibrator, and an amplified loudspeaker, and that's it. It has been tuned for this aircraft, and, as far as we can tell, it works okay, on the ground at least. Now, we want you to give it an air test Okay?" "Super, let's do that!" replied John.

He taxied the Moth to the takeoff point with the noise canceller turned off. Even without it, he could tell at once the engine was even quieter than it had previously been. He turned the device on, and immediately the hum of the engine faded; he could still feel the slight vibrations inherent in even the most perfectly balanced four-cylinder engine. Opening the throttle to check the magnetos was almost alarming—apart from the indication on the rpm gauge and an increase in slipstream, there was no noise at all. Completing the takeoff checklist, he opened the throttle to max power, and the Moth accelerated smoothly and soundlessly away. With the tail off the ground and slipstream increasing, the aircraft was uncannily quiet. John thought to himself, *This is what it must be like to be deaf.* Even the normal rumble of the wheels bumping over the grass strip was absent. He eased the Moth into the dark, silver night sky, and turned 180 degrees left, climbing to two hundred feet. Levelling at that height, he turned farther left and flew directly over the hangar. As he passed over the entrance, he could just make out the figures of the ground party standing by the entrance. He partly closed the throttle then rapidly opened up again to full power. Not a sound. This was uncanny. Climbing to one thousand feet and maintaining full power, he accelerated then dove the Moth down to two hundred feet. The normal vibrations from the canvas covering, the rigging, and the slipstream at high speed were present but not a sound. This was unreal! He turned back again to cross the hangar from the rear. Approaching it, he dropped down to rooftop level and flew over it and the crew outside, and then pulled back up to two hundred feet to make an approach and landing.

Arriving back at the hangar, he cut the engine, switched everything off, and climbed out. He was met by an enthusiastic group, led by Ginger. The questions began: "How did it perform?" "What could you hear?" "How were the cylinder head temperatures?" "Did it fly okay?" and so on. When he finished replying, Johnny asked Bill, "Did you hear much from the aircraft as I buzzed you?" "Not a thing," Ginger butted in excitedly. "As a matter of fact, after you had taxied away everything went quiet; we were looking for you getting airborne but didn't hear or see a thing. When you buzzed us, we just felt the slipstream like a sudden gust of wind. The shadow, or what appeared to be a shadow, swept over us and was gone. Like a bloody ghost! It was unnerving, I can tell you! Christ, it was like someone walking over your grave!" One of the others cut in, "We didn't hear or see you land either, or taxi back. Just heard you climbing out of the cockpit then you appeared out of the shadow. It was unreal!" Paddy then cut in. "Well, Johnny, m' boy, it seems the evening has been a success. Let's go and get a pint to celebrate!"

That week, John flew two night missions over to the other side without a hitch. The reaction of his passengers had been quiet amazement. As one put it, "The silence was deafening! I could hear the traffic on the roads below and a church clock chiming the hour!" For the rest of the time, normal squadron flying went on smoothly and without incident. One evening Paddy appeared in the bar and suggested that they go to his room to chat. Settling John down in a chair with a glass of beer, he said, "We've caught the bugger, Johnny!"

"Not our big leak, by any chance?"

"Yes indeed. It happened yesterday in London. We had set the trap very carefully. When you did your last two missions for us, we put out two different pickup locations. They were passed to the two people concerned in the office there. However, at local level here, we changed the rendezvous sites. Only you, I, and the team on the ground over the border knew about those. Anyway, we then had the two fake sites monitored for the time you were supposed to arrive. Both the sites were swarming with troops at the appointed time, and confusion reigned, it would seem. Of course they all eventually went away sadly disappointed. Our masters in London rapidly interrogated the two individuals concerned and quickly discovered which one was guilty. He is now enjoying an extended stay in the countryside spilling the beans!" John laughed and said, "Serves the sod right; I hope they make the bastard suffer!"

Later that month Bob Newton, the squadron adjutant, approached John. "It seems your gunnery instructors course at Leconfield has come up, Johnny. Due to start Monday the second of November; you'll need to be there by Sunday the first. Now, do you want to take some leave prior to going on it?"

He applied for three weeks leave prior to that and passed the information on to Paddy. Two days later, he had his instructions. "Go home on leave; have a few days off. Then hire a car, drive down to a certain pub in a village near Crawley, and be there by the eleventh of October for 1:00 p.m. Go in civilian clothes. Expect to be there for two weeks, and then return home for a week or so before going up to Leconfield for the instructors course, which ends on December the eighteenth. You can go home for Christmas but report back to Celle by December 30. The squadron is off to Sylt again on New Year's Day for its air-to-air training session. Not a word to anyone about your movements or activities. You are simply touring around."

FOURTEEN

Sunday the eleventh of October found John parking an unremarkable Austin 16, which he had borrowed from his old friend Harry, in front of the selected pub, alongside a rather smart Riley 2½-litre saloon. He entered the pub and went left into the lounge bar. The sole customer was his old acquaintance, Geoff Sanders, who greeted him. "You're about one minute early. Nice timing!" "Well, we aim to please," John retorted. "Hope you're buying the first round! Mine's a pint of bitter, please."

A little later, after some small talk, Geoff said, "We'd best be off then. Why don't you follow me at a gentle pace, and you can take in the glorious scenery on the way." From the village they drove down a side road for a mile or so before turning into a driveway, the approaches to which were well concealed by high hedgerows. Set back a little were large and very sturdy ornamental gates flanked by impressive stone pillars. From the pillars on each side, a high and very secure fence was barely visible concealed behind the hedgerows. Just inside the gates stood a gatekeeper's cottage. Before they came to a halt, a figure appeared from the cottage dressed in civilian clothes. He looked hard at Geoff's car, gave a nod of acknowledgement, and the gates opened quite quickly. The cars drove through, and John noticed that the gates closed very smartly behind them. The long, winding driveway led them to the front of a rambling old country mansion, which appeared to have undergone many alterations and additions during its undoubtedly long existence. The driveway was not typically surfaced with gravel but was entirely asphalted. They drove past the front and turned into a large courtyard between the house and a formidable stable block, again, asphalted, and pulled into two marked parking spaces amid several other vehicles.

Inside the rear hallway, John followed Geoff into a small but well-appointed office. "Come in and sit yourself down." Geoff motioned to an easy chair by the fireplace; before joining John in a similar chair, he opened a drinks cabinet. "What can I get you? Gin, scotch, or something else?" "I think a scotch with soda would be grand, thanks!"

After the drinks had been attended to, Geoff began. "You are probably wondering what the hell this is all about, so let me fill you in. Here, in this building, we can talk openly and freely without interruption or being overheard. This is important because what I am about to tell you is for your ears only. It will be highly confidential and will not go outside this room. Now, first, the background. From the results of your initial aircrew selection board at Hornchurch, we have been keeping an eye on your progress and, at the risk of flattering you, have been impressed. Needless to say, there have been extensive inquiries into your past, and we probably know more about you than you know yourself! Right; we have in mind a very special future mapped out for you, and I shall give you the general outline, from which you will gather the importance of the role we have in mind for you. It's a long road ahead, fraught with difficulties no doubt, and will entail moments of peril not associated with flying necessarily! So before I proceed further, I have to remind you that you are bound by the Official Secrets Act and all it implies. This you know already, but what you will learn, should you accept the role, is classified top secret. Do you fully understand? And do you have any reservations before I proceed?"

John pondered for a moment before replying. His mind was racing thorough all the implications at enormous speed. He mentally thought of a hundred possibilities and, at the same time, had a very distinct feeling that maybe this was what his mission in life might just be. The conclusion reached after a long minute was, *Why not, it should make life interesting*, and he took the plunge. "No, I have no reservations; pray continue. Let me know what I'm in for!"

"Right you are, then," Geoff began. "What you will be is an agent working for the military intelligence, with a direct input to the Joint Intelligence Committee, otherwise known as the JIC. You will actually be reporting directly through me, or my successors, to the chief of defence intelligence. We shall also be your directors. You have already been doing this on your moonlight wanderings and have greatly impressed our lords and masters. Had your activities been in the public eye, you would, by now, have been awarded a decoration, in fact an AFC, but that is not possible. You see, at this point no one on the other side knows of you; in fact, apart from a handful of people, no one in the air force knows what you have been doing either! We want to keep it that way. You see, the other side scans all our newspapers and keeps a close eye on all the officers in all of our services, including our Ministry of Intelligence, and are very aware of their activities. You are under the radar, so to speak, and we intend keeping it that way. Any questions so far?" John shook his head. "No, please carry on; I'd like to hear all you have to say."

"Very well. Officially, to the world at large and to the RAF, you are simply a pilot, and that's just how we want to keep it. We need your curious flying skills for what we intend your future role to be. Your being a military pilot will actually be your cover for your other activities. I am not trying to flatter you. It's a simple statement of fact. We shall be putting you through an extensive schooling in what we call 'trade craft,' not all at once, but just a little at a time. This will be done discreetly, without the knowledge of anyone except our small group. Some of it will be regular service courses, the sort you have done with the SAS, for example. However, the rest of it will be surreptitious. Of course, and again I caution you, not a word to a soul about this; lives, including your own, depend upon it. At the end of the day there will be no official recognition for what you do. Certain protections will be afforded to you, *but* should you be discovered by our enemies whilst 'undercover,' we would officially deny all knowledge of your activities. Hence, you will become a 'deniable asset.'"

John nodded, "I do understand all of that, fully. I have the feeling that I will not be bored with it, Geoff."

"Make no mistake, it won't be easy. You'll have to get used to lying a lot to your nearest and dearest in order to maintain your cover, and it will require a lot of dedication, sacrifice, and self-control. We shall do all we possibly can to support you, but at the end of the day you will have to rely upon yourself," Geoff explained. "Right, then. We'll get started.

There's a couple of forms to read and sign, and then we shall get started. This house is a school, and for the rest of this week we run you through briefings and some essential little courses. At the weekend, go home, then go on to Leconfield on Sunday to start your gunnery instructors course, okay, that part, of course, is strictly legit! For your cover, you can tell your people, if they ask, that you've been visiting an old friend from your training days in Rhodesia. Get used to being deceptive without showing it. Always make up a cover story that is as near to the truth as possible, then, stick with it! Got it? Oh!, by the way, it's good to have you aboard, and good luck for all that lies ahead for us."

At the end of the week, John returned to his home on the Friday afternoon. Calling in at Harry's garage, he turned in the Austin 16 and collected his own particular transportation, a relatively new Vincent Black Shadow, series C motorcycle. The Vincent was the fastest production motorbike yet produced, capable of nearly 125 mph, and could cruise effortlessly at any speed up to 100 mph. This particular one had been tweaked somewhat by the addition of the racing 'black lightning' cams, larger carburettors, and E7/8 pistons, giving a higher compression ratio. The rear drive sprockets had been changed to a forty-five-tooth rear wheel and twenty-two-tooth gearbox sprocket, giving an overall top gear ratio of 3.27:1, a little higher than the standard 3.5:1. The front brakes already had the finned drums; and the racing, cast electron back plates with cooling air scoops had been installed.

These assorted 'tweaks' had raised the top speed to 140 mph, with effortless cruising at any speed above 50 mph. Harry had also procured for John a set of crash bars that Vincent had designed for police use. These fitted the unique "frameless" configuration of the Vincent, and John had fitted a pair of detachable leg shields for bad weather riding to the crash bars. In concert with these, he had devised a very individual one-piece windshield air deflector, smaller than the average windshield, which one could see over, not through. Mounted behind the Girdaulic fork assembly, it was light in weight and incorporated handlebar shields, giving protection to the rider from the hurricane-force slipstream riding at speeds way beyond 70 mph. The final modification was a special seat support, which isolated the dual seat from the rear suspension. This incorporated a pannier frame to which, when not carrying a pillion passenger, two normal medium size suitcases could be strapped on;

a smaller overnight case or briefcase could be attached behind the pillion position. Slightly stronger rear springs had been fitted to the suspension units to accommodate the higher loadings. This whole rear assembly had been fabricated by Harry's chief mechanic, Dennis, who was highly skilled at this type of work. It was made from Reynolds 531 tubing and was, thus, light in weight but strong. The result of these modifications was a very swift machine, which could go from A to B anywhere in Great Britain faster than any other vehicle in virtually any weather, carrying the solo rider and a sufficiency of dress and uniform needs for any occasion. In all, an ideal steed for a young, unattached flying officer.

One of Harry's customers had ordered the Vincent new, and after riding for a very short time decided that it was "too fast for owner." Sadly, shortly thereafter he had been killed whilst riding another of his three motorcycles, this one a comparatively tame and docile Douglas 350. His distraught parents simply wanted to dispose of the remaining two bikes to someone who could appreciate them and had gone to Harry. In turn, Harry had mentioned an impecunious young RAF pilot friend of his who really did need, and would appreciate, such a machine. One who, furthermore, would be unlikely to come to harm on it. The parents had met John briefly, and in an act of great generosity, had presented him the Black Shadow as a gift, refusing any form of payment.

On the Sunday morning, he set off quite early to ride up to Leconfield, near Beverley, in Yorkshire. He had packed his bags and prepared and fuelled the bike the previous afternoon, and after a very light breakfast he had donned his riding gear for cold weather. An RAF "Irvin" flying jacket and matching trousers over his casual whipcord trousers and Fair Isle sweater. A pair of silk under gloves with a pair of wool-lined leather gauntlets for the hands and, to complete the ensemble, a very new crash helmet from Cromwell. This company was currently developing a protective flying helmet for the RAF, which was to become standard issue later. John's helmet was similar in style, and it incorporated the sliding visor, which gave complete protection to the eyes and nose. This protective clothing, in conjunction with the protection installed on the bike, made long-distance, nonstop, high-speed riding a reasonable and very practical means of travel for a single person.

He mounted up at precisely 6:00 a.m. and set out on his carefully planned route, avoiding the larger cities and towns wherever possible. Heading north from the village on the A435 through Measham to Ashby-De-La-Zouch, then off on the B5324 after Coleorton, and following that until joining the A46 just after passing RAF Wymeswold. These were all roads he knew intimately, and he made good time in the dark, the way well lit by the Miller headlamp. Turning onto the A46, dawn was beginning to rise to herald a clear, dry autumn morning with good visibility. On this old Roman road, with its long straight sections, he could open the throttle and begin to fly. The Vincent was characterised by a very distinct riding position. The rider poised higher than on other motorcycles. The short, straight handlebars give the rider a slight forward lean, balancing him against the slipstream. Johnny had tailored his riding position exactly, with the very adjustable footrests and controls afforded by the Vincent. At 70 to 100 mph, everything came into balance. Neatly tucked in behind the minimal windshield, there was no strain on the arms or wrists from the formidable headwind; he became one with the bike. The mechanical noise of the valve gear fell silent, obscured by the wind. The magnificent 998 cc V-twin engine fell into its steady, smooth rhythm, loping along at an easy pace, with great reservoirs of power still at hand.

John found that all these factors would come together and produce a tactile sense of euphoria that was so similar to low flying in an aircraft. The control of the machine was not accomplished by conscious operation of the controls, but more by gentle pressures. Harsh movements would upset the balances involved. Indeed, many of the horror stories of motorcycles getting out of control and developing steering wobbles, known as "tank slappers," were caused by rider-induced errors. The control operation became subconscious and automatic, as with flying an aircraft, allowing him to concentrate on the road ahead, scanning to the horizon for potential hazards and planning his moves well in advance.

These techniques, when employed as a matter of course and normal practice, allow an expert to cover long distances, quite safely, at very high speeds. The normal traffic of the time was pedestrian by comparison. Most cars pottered along at speeds not much greater than 45 mph. Lorries at 25 to 40 mph. Few cars could exceed the magic "ton," 100 mph, at that time. The only two cars in current production that could do so comfortably were the Jaguar XK120 and the Bentley Continental. When one is cruising along at 100 mph, ordinary vehicles present no problem in overtaking. To all intents and purposes, they might well be parked obstructions, which one passed in an instant. Should one be faced with oncoming traffic and have to slow, the four brake drums of the Vincent were most effective, and the immense acceleration available ensured that cruising speed was swiftly regained. In towns and villages a 30 mph speed limit applied; outside the built-up areas, speed was unrestricted in those days so one was able to fully utilise all of the immense potential of this mile-eater. The miles flew by as John passed Newark and joined the Main A1 great north road to Bawtry; traffic had increased a little, but Johnny sped along with easy grace, well into the rhythm and onward pace. From here, he departed the A1 for A614 to cross the Humber River at Goole. After Goole, Howden was swiftly passed and on to Newport, where he swung onto the B1230 for Beverley. There joining the main street in town, he turned north again onto the A164, passing under the old Norman archway building at the North Gate on the final two and a half-mile leg of his journey to Leconfield.

Invigorated after his exhilarating ride at a very high average speed over almost deserted roads, he had covered the 103 miles from his home in just under two hours. He signed in at the mess and was shown to his room. At just after eight o'clock, he wandered into the dining room in search of breakfast. The room had but one other diner at this early hour. As was usual in RAF messes, most young officers were sleeping off the effects of the weekend partying, so there was nothing unusual about this fact. John went over and sat at the same large refectory dining table, across from the other person and not too close, not wishing to intrude upon the man's rapt attention to a newspaper.

A waiter approached and took John's order for breakfast whilst pouring him a cup of tea. In the silence that followed, John politely and quietly said, "Good morning" to his companion. He was answered by a grunt and a quiver of the paper. He then strolled over to the toaster set on a side table and stuck two pieces of bread in the machine. Whilst waiting for the toast to cook, he took the opportunity to look over his silent neighbor. Rather surprisingly, this officer presented a strange and unkempt appearance. His tousled red hair was embedded with bits of straw; he was unshaven and bore traces of muck and dirt on his face and clothing. The latter was a voluminous and filthy, worn and tatty old Harris Tweed jacket that had had a hard life. The elbows and cuffs were bound with leather, which had been abraded through over time. He wore an old and equally scruffy pair of corduroy trousers, and, to complete the ensemble, his footwear was a pair of incredible filthy old rubber Wellington boots.

John sat down and sipped his tea and then watched with fascination as his fellow diner relinquished a hand from the newspaper, took a piece of buttered toast, dipped it into a runny egg yolk on his breakfast plate, and then proceeded to stuff it into his jacket's voluminous side pocket. A little while later this bizarre procedure took place again and then again. Eventually curiosity could be contained no longer. At the risk of appearing forward, John politely and quietly inquired, "Sir, do pardon my curiosity, but just why are you putting pieces of eggy toast into your pocket? I'm intrigued."

"Well, I'm feeding my ferrets, of course, you bloody fool!" came the reply.

Thus, John met one of the flight commanders for the gunnery course. An intriguing personality, although somewhat lacking in social graces, Buchanan was admired by the local populous and was famous throughout Fighter Command for his wildfowling abilities, poaching skills, and nefarious activities. The happy result being that the dining to be had in the Leconfield mess was reckoned to be the finest in the Royal Air Force at that time. Later that day, in the little bar at the back of the mess, whilst having a drink before dinner, who should walk in but John's old friend and jet instructor at Valley, Bill Edwards. It transpired that Bill was the other flight commander and that John, with his fellow course mates, would be on Bill's flight. An impromptu reunion then began, and the following morning saw some rather hungover pilots sitting down for their introductory briefing and first day of lectures.

The course that ensued was fairly intensive but relaxed. All of John's classmates were experienced pilots, and all had been the best at gunnery on their respective squadrons. As a result, there were some colourful characters amongst them. This became apparent later that week. On the Thursday evening, the mess held a dining-in night to welcome the new arrivals. The evening started sedately with all the senior officers of the permanent staff and the guest of honour mixing with the crowd of junior officers. Again, old acquaintances were renewed over drinks before moving in to dinner. The meal itself was superb, featuring seven courses that included trout, pheasant and jugged hare. The meal passed quietly enough, and prior to coffee being served, the toasts to the queen and others was observed. Following this, the president of the Mess Committee, the PMC, introduced the guest of honour, who happened to be the local justice of the peace, who was also the owner of the land the airfield stood upon, as well as a fair amount of the surrounding landscape. His opening remarks set everyone at ease and created gales of laughter when he said that he always enjoyed eating with the RAF in this mess, if for no better reason than he could enjoy his own game, superbly cooked and served, thanks to a certain officer who would remain nameless. Seemingly, the JP added, it also kept his gamekeepers on the ball in their fervent but vain attempts to catch the dreaded nameless person, Buchanan (of the ferrets), in the act of poaching the aforesaid game! In an atmosphere of warm companionship, the diners retired from the dining room to the modest but cosy bar.

This structure had been built at the rear of the prewar mess building. Prior to the war, all drinks used to be served in the anteroom and brought in by a waiter. With the vast increase of officers during hostilities, this practice was impractical, and so the bar had been added. It was essentially a standard RAF wooden accommodation building grafted onto the rear main corridor. Over the years it acquired a thatched straw canopy over the bar itself, which was located at the far end of the room. Close by, and to the right of the entrance, a splendid brick fireplace and chimney had been built. In the chillier days of autumn and winter, this provided a pleasant warmth to the room. It provided a place for the senior officers, on an occasion such as this evening, to stand around warming their backsides in front of the blaze of wood logs used for fuel.

The loud buzz of the contented, happy, postprandial group was suddenly shattered with a very loud explosion accompanied by clouds of soot, ash, sparks, and cinders erupting from the fireplace, covering the senior group in a spectacular manner. This afforded a great opportunity to the younger officers grouped around the bar to immediately rush to the aid of their direly afflicted seniors. With great presence of mind, they were able to douse the singed and smouldering afflicted with pints of beer, which they had in hand. Of course, this extinguished the conflagration but left the recipients of this worthy action very bedraggled indeed. They left, almost to a man, to repair the damage to their clothing and wash away the dirt from their faces, swearing to hunt down the perpetrator of this foul deed. Those remaining continued their carousing into the early hours, the consensus being that it was the best dining-in night experienced in a very long time!

The following morning, at the daily met briefing, the class of students was given an ultimatum; either the culprit would own up to this prank or the whole class would suffer the same fate in store for him. The person, or persons, concerned would do so before Monday morning; if not, the whole class would be confined to their rooms except to dine, attend classes, and fly. In the meantime, they were reminded, there was to be C in C's Fighter Command annual unit inspection the following Wednesday, and everything had to be immaculate for that occasion, including the aircraft.

The aircraft were the standard Meteor Mk.8 fighter and were finished in silver paint. In the course of time, this paintwork became dull and dirty from rain, smog, and the black soot from the four 20 mm cannons mounted in the nose. Therefore, these aircraft had to be clean, bright, and shiny for this important event. What better use could the course members be put to but cleaning the aforesaid aircraft? Particularly as next Monday and Tuesday had very poor, foggy weather forecast, and it was unlikely that any flying could be done! Thus, their fate was sealed.

Over the weekend, the culprit made his obeyance to the PMC, who immediately confined him to his quarters for the duration of the course except for classes and flying. The word quickly spread that the rest of his classmates were off the hook; however, the aircraft still needed to be cleaned. This was a more difficult task than expected. Work had begun on a dull, foggy Monday morning, and progress was slow. By the end of the day, with only one day left before the big event, John and his classmates suggested that in view of the very limited visibility forecast for the inspection on Wednesday, and taking into consideration the fact that the parade would take place in front of the aircraft, not much of the aircraft could be seen from the reviewing stand. Therefore, why not just clean the front of the aircraft? This would then be achievable. This solution was grudgingly accepted, and the parade took place as scheduled. On the day, the prediction proved correct. It was so foggy that the band leading the parade became disoriented and marched past the reviewing stand on the wrong side, then disappeared from view altogether. From the reviewing stand, only the noses of the Meteors were visible beyond the ranks of the parade. As the inspection of the parade was about to begin, the light rain gave way to a steadily increasing downpour. The C in C declared this was a ridiculous waste of time and suggested that the parade be dismissed and that all the officers should retire to the mess bar, where he would like to meet some of them.

This sensible suggestion was rapidly enacted, and, in due course, a roaring party ensued. During the event, it was found that the perpetrator of the exploding fireplace was a dedicated young man. His squadron commander had suffered other minor episodes with him and had begun to think he had a pyromaniac on his hands. Certainly, he had someone dedicated and fascinated in the art of explosive warfare! It was rumoured also that he contrived to send the said young officer away on as many courses as possible to achieve some degree of peace and quiet on his squadron! Thus, exposed to the unfeeling gaze of the gunnery school, he was exiled for the duration.

In the weeks that followed, he did keep a very low, solicitous profile. For exercise he had taken to cycling about the airfield in the twilight hours, and he kept himself very much to himself. However, the night porter on the mess staff reported that he had seen a ghostly figure pacing the mess corridors at night, flitting silently about the place, and that he had seen a batlike creature flying silently around in the anteroom and dining room. These reports were not taken seriously for it was known that the night porter was fond of his tipple, and there were no other credible witnesses.

November rolled on into December, and the course progressed. The Christmas season was fast approaching, and many parties were held in the local area. Johnny was enjoying the whole scene enormously. He had been off to his home stamping grounds on several weekends, riding with a couple of hunts, the Quorn and the Atherstone, and seeing his old friends and acquaintances, the Black Shadow providing swift transportation back and forth. He also made the acquaintance of two young ladies during this time, one in Beverley and another at the Derby Flying Club. These were both very attractive and most presentable. Sadly, John discovered, both were very intent on the major form of commitment, namely marriage, as soon as possible. This commitment, he felt, he was not ready for at this stage in his life, and so he then made it his policy to be seen with as many young ladies as possible, a course of action that his avid persuers found upsetting, as did their families. He began to find this hyperactive social life somewhat fatiguing, and the thought of returning to the quieter but exciting persuits in darker Germany, a comforting thought.

As the course drew to a close, a final dining-out night was arranged to celebrate its success. This was held again on the Thursday evening. The following day all the course members would depart to return to their units or on leave to spend their Christmas with their families. Again, the members gathered in the bar arrayed in black tie formality. The dinner was superb, as to be expected at Leconfield; the wines likewise, in excellence and quantity. The guest of honour was a rather famous fighter pilot, long retired from the service but a well-known wit and humorist, much in demand for after-dinner speaking. The dinner buzzed happily along, and a very relaxed group was brought to order by the PMC calling for Mr. Vice to propose the Loyal Toast. The queen's health was drunk, and the PMC banged the gavel to begin the speeches to follow. Whereupon, a strange event took place.

It must be explained that the dining tables had been arranged in the form of an extended U. The head table, at the bottom of the U, seating the president, the guest, and the senior officers facing the entrance doors at the far end of the room. The rest of the diners were arranged each side of the U, and all eyes were focussed toward the head table and the PMC. There was a moment of quiet, which fell to a hush, as they saw a look of puzzlement, then horror, cross the features of the PMC. His mouth fell open, and he stood, open mouthed, eyes boggling. As the assembled company stared at him, they heard, coming from behind them, from the vicinity of the entrance doors, a sibilant whirring sound. They looked around to see the remarkable sight of a very large model aircraft, with a wingspan of three feet or so, flying steadily up the aisle between the tables toward the head table. The whirring sound was produced by the propellor, driven by a rubber band of some considerable power. Even more impressive was the very large "thunderflash" it carried under its fuselage with a fizzing igniter cord protruding from its rear end. No one moved; no one spoke. Six feet before arriving at the head table, directly in front of PMC, it exploded on cue with a deafening bang and a mass of red paper confetti and aircraft parts.

The assembled throng was silent for a moment, and then the great uproar of amusement broke out. Shrieks of joyous laughter, banging on the table, and hoots of merriment pealed throughout for the next few minutes. The PMC, rising to the occasion, entered into the spirit of the gesture; his face broke into wreaths of smiles, he banged the gavel again and introduced the guest of honour before collapsing helpless with laughter, knocking over his wineglass as he did so. To cap it all, the headwaiter had pulled back the PMC's chair as he had risen to speak. In the confusion that had transpired since, the waiter, befuddled by the events, had neglected to replace the chair. Thus, the fated PMC disappeared from sight below the table as he sat down on the vacant space.

The guest of honour, recovering well from the hilarious events, rose to his feet and gave a splendidly amusing speech, full of wit, humour, and unlikely tales, which perfectly complimented the affair. He praised the ingenuity of the whole evening, the gay spirits of the young fighter pilots, and the fact that they were carrying on the best traditions of the service. Later, back in the bar, he insisted upon being introduced to each one of them, including the exiled "blaster Supreme."

John spent the following morning saying farewell to his friends and the ground crew who had helped him during the last two months, and then packing the Vincent for his departure. He left after lunch, and after a swift passage, returned to his home in good time to unpack and change for the evening ahead with his old friends Eric, Bill, and Jeevo, who would be having a noisy reunion over the weekend and the Christmas week that followed.

FIFTEEN

Sunday, December 27, 1953.

John had ridden over to the village of Austrey, where his friend Eric lived. They had met at the village pub, The Bird in Hand, for a quiet lunchtime pint. This was a favorite meeting place for them. The publican, Gordon, said to John as he served him, "There was a telephone call for you about fifteen minutes ago; the chap said he needed to get in touch with you. That was all; he left this number for you to call him back. If you like, you can use my phone in the sitting room; it's private there."

"Thanks, Gordon, I'll do that if you don't mind," John replied, and then went through to the private sitting room. He dialled the number, and the voice answering enquired, "Whose calling, please?" John gave his name, and after a few moments, Geoff's voice came on the line.

"John, sorry to intrude on your few days break, but we do need to see you to discuss plans. Look, I'm going to be up in your area tomorrow, staying over at RAF Wymeswold. Any chance you could meet me over there?"

"Of course. What time will you be there?"

"I'll be driving up in the morning; expect to be there by lunchtime. Perhaps we could meet in the mess there?"

"Right ho! I'll be there. Are you buying?"

Next morning, John headed out on the Vincent, arriving at the Wymeswold mess at just on twelve. As he turned into the mess car park, he saw Geoff getting his bags from the trunk of his car. Pulling up alongside, he switched off the Vincent's engine and was greeted by Geoff saying, "Immaculate timing. I wish everyone would be so prompt." John quickly retorted, "I think I've got the right date as well, by the look of things!"

A while later, in the privacy of his room, Geoff briefed John. "There have been a few developments, and I wanted to get you up to speed. As you know, you'll be going from UK directly to Sylt, to arrive there on the first of January. What we want you to do is to leave here a day early and go to Celle. We've booked you a VIP room on the Blue Train. Get some sleep onboard. At Celle, Paddy will meet you and take you directly to the Bat Hangar. We need you to do one quick flit across the line. When you've done the trip, Paddy will take you back to the hotel. You will then board the train the following morning to get up to Sylt. That will get you there on time with no one the wiser. Okay?" John nodded an assent.

"Now," Geoff continued, "looking down the road at some future plans. In February, you will be sent over to Farnborough on an RAF project, 'Fighter Cockpit Design.' Your boss has already put your name down for it, so act surprised when he tells you. It's intended to be a two-week seminar, and you will apply for two weeks of leave as well. As soon as the seminar has finished, go on over to the 'Manor,' where your presence is needed for some more indoctrination, which will take about a week. When that's over, go on home for the rest of the time before returning to Celle. Okay so far?"

"Yes, but can you tell me what the seminar is about? It sounds very interesting."

"Well, it's not my line of country exactly, but, as I understand it, it's something to do with helping to design the ideal fighter cockpit. Beyond that, I know not! Oh! Yes, there is one more thing. All this flitting to and fro is an awful lot of train and boat time. We think we have a better idea. As you probably know, here at Wymeswold, the only resident squadron is 504, City of Nottingham, which is an auxiliary reserve squadron; there is also an MU, that's a maintenance unit, which happens to suit our purposes well. The plan is that from time to time you'll get a message that you are needed here; we shall supply a cover story for you. You will then bring over an aircraft here to Wymeswold and will return to Celle a few days later, either in the same aircraft or with a replacement. We realize this airfield is very convenient for your home, and you could keep your motorcycle here if you like. We know how handy it is for your zipping around the country on. This is a very central location for anywhere in this country."

John thought for a moment. "Well, I love the idea of being able to fly to and fro; the rail and boat trip is bloody awful, but I'm a bit uncertain of leaving the bike here unless I can lock it safely away somewhere. It's what might be described as a 'valuable and attractive item.'" Geoff replied, "We've thought of that already. There's a small hut next to one of the hangars. It's empty and has been allocated to me. I have here a padlock and two keys. You can have one, and I'll keep the other. You'll be able to safely store the Vincent there. It has been painted with a number of 'Security, Keep Out' signs."

It was early evening when John stepped off the Blue Train at Celle, having had the most comfortable journey he had yet experienced, and he felt well rested. Paddy met him on the platform and whisked him off through an unmarked door, then through the building and out onto the street, where his car was parked. They drove directly to the Bat Hangar. On the way, Paddy briefed him on the flight ahead that night.

"This one is a tricky one," Paddy began. "The client is of vital importance to us. He's a German scientist who the Ruskis roped in at the end of the war. He has managed to slip the bonds and is actually 'on the run.' Fortunately, he is with an agent of ours, safe for the moment; but the word is out on him. We've arranged this pickup for tonight, and we feel it's probably a good rendezvous location. It's farther into 'The Zone' than we've been before, but we don't want to risk moving him again. Too much at stake! Of course, as you will no doubt have noticed, the weather is fair to lousy! And it is not forecast to get any better. The location is near to a little town, name of Bismark, no less. The nearest large town is Stendal; that's to the west of Berlin. I'll show you the area map when we get to the hangar."

On arrival there, the crew had the "Bat" all ready to go. After a very through briefing, John climbed into his warm flying clothing, checked the aircraft over, strapped into the cockpit, and started the mission. Once airborne, he set course for the first of a carefully chosen route. The weather was not good—cloud base at about fifteen hundred feet;

visibility around a mile or so, forecast to deteriorate as a front approached from the west. He picked up the first turning point without difficulty, and the rest of his outbound journey was uneventful, with a slight bonus that the farther east he flew the weather improved. As he flew along in the unnatural silence of the Bat, he went over the landing field brief in his mind. The area itself was to the west of Stendal. Beyond that town lay the village of Bismark, and again to the west lay the hamlet of Poritz. Northwest of Poritz sat another hamlet, Butterhorst. Between these two hamlets lay a flat plain irrigated by two ditches, which ran in straight lines. They formed a fork to the northwest of the chosen field and were fed by another ditch leading to a tributary of the river Elbe. Crossing the two canals, which were aligned northeast to southwest, was a farm track, which also gave access to an old farmhouse that stood surrounded by gardens and trees. This house lay to the southeast of the landing strip, which, John had been informed, was always ploughed from east to west and had a very smooth, well-drained surface.

Reaching the end of the last leg of his flight, he spotted the initial point for his approach. He checked his time and saw he was about thirty seconds early. Although there was thin cloud cover, the water feature stood out very clearly. Then he spotted a darker area ahead, slightly to the left, which must be the house in the trees. He throttled back to approach speed then, with his left hand, took his small but powerful flashlight from his leg pocket, pointed it straight ahead, and flashed it once. He was to expect just three short flashes in return. Any more, or less, was a wave-off signal, and the mission was to be aborted. It felt like an eternity, but then he saw the three flashes in reply.

He landed and slowed quite quickly. The moment he stopped, he gave one flash with the blue taillight then reached down into his map pocket for his Browning Hi-Power. He actioned the slide, slipped off the safety catch, and held the gun against the side of the fuselage at the ready. About a minute past, then he saw two shadowy figures struggling toward the aircraft. As they neared, he could see one was limping very badly and was being half carried by the other person. They reached the wingtip on his left side, and it seemed that his assistance would be needed. They came up to the cockpit side, and John gave his password challenge. The injured person gave the correct response and added "Danke!" In an instant, Johnny realized something was amiss, and his finger tightened on the trigger, taking up the first pressure. The helper mumbled something and then pushed the passenger to one side and started to pull a gun from his pocket, saying "You are under ahhhhh…!" and then fell backwards to the ground. John had already pulled the trigger twice, the "double tap." The first of the two 9 mm rounds struck the man in the chest a little to the right of the sternum, entered the right ventricle of the heart, and then penetrated the descending aorta before hitting the spine between two vertebrae, severing the spinal cord, where it came to rest, paralysing the man. The other round struck a little higher and to the right, striking a rib, and then tumbling as it tore into the left atrium, exiting into the upper loop of the aorta before slowing and coming to rest against the left shoulder blade. Either shot would have killed almost instantly.

John slipped the safety catch on and stuffed the gun back into its pocket. Simultaneously he released his safety harness, stepped out of the cockpit, and helped the wounded man up into the front cockpit, quickly strapping him in and pulling the helmet over his head. Climbing back into the rear cockpit, he smartly opened the throttle and rolled into the takeoff run; on his left, he saw movement at the side of the field. As he accelerated, he heard several shots fired as the figures began running towards the aircraft. At full throttle, only a whisper could be heard from the engine and propeller, but the acceleration was rapid. He could see the line of the canal ahead, marked by a few trees—plenty of room for takeoff. At about fifty knots, the port undercarriage wheel hit a very solid object of some sort that John had not seen. There was an almighty wrench accompanied by a loud *bang*, and the aircraft slewed to the left. He countered with a bootful of right rudder. The aircraft bounced once, and he caught it, and then he gently finessed the machine into the air. They were flying, but barely! Having staggered up to two hundred feet, John levelled off and accelerated, heaving a sigh of relief.

As the Bat gathered speed, he could not fail to notice that some object was attached to the port undercarriage and was flapping around in the slipstream. Not only was it creating a lot of drag, it was also hitting the trailing edge of the port wing, doing it no good whatsoever. From what he could see, it was some sort of metal farm implement, left in the field by some idle sod or the other. He pondered what to do. Quickly realizing that not much could be done, he turned his attention to the poor man in the front cockpit. "Can you hear me? Do you speak English?" John asked.

"Yes," came the strained reply. "Thank you. Is everything okay? Can we fly?" he questioned in good English.

"Well, we seem to be staggering along in some fashion," John remarked. "We'll just have to make the best of it. Now, what's the matter with you? Are you hurt badly?"

"I am hurting, yes! They stopped us on the road here, shot my escort, and then beat me badly, making me give them the password. It is some sort of pain in my lower abdomen, on the right side. I think it might be my, how do you say, ummh, appendix?"

"Oh, I see. Well, if you can hold out for an hour we'll get you safely to a doctor. Try to relax and don't talk unless you have to. I shall keep talking to you, however. Just try to stay awake," John encouraged.

Turning his attention to the flight plan, he looked ahead and spotted his first turning point on the homeward journey. He slowly climbed to five hundred feet then a little more, to one thousand. A few spots of rain splattered on the small windscreen as they burbled along. He noticed that the turbulence from the flapping appendage was obviously outside the parameters of the sound-cancelling device. In fact, it was creating a very unpleasant rattling noise. Furthermore, the excessive drag had reduced the airspeed by a considerable factor. This, in its turn, would create a fuel consumption problem. John pondered all of this as they staggered along.

Reaching the next turning point, the rain had begun in earnest. At one thousand feet, the aircraft was in and out of the bottom of the clouds, and some turbulence was making itself felt. Suddenly the Bat hit an air pocket and bounced heavily; this caused the unwanted object to tear itself away from the aircraft, and, to his horror, John saw it break away, taking with it the port wheel and most of its supporting struts. As it did so, some flailing part of it struck the tailplane. The immediate effect was a welcome acceleration. The problem was, how much control damage had it caused? Gently he tried the elevators. *Thank God*, he thought, *they seem to work okay. Now let's try the rudder. Yes, that doesn't seem to be jammed in any way; all I've got to worry about now is finding my way back and then landing the sodding thing!'*

The weather now was much worse. He descended to five hundred feet in very heavy rain. It was very cold and dark. The thought of possible icing crossed his mind, but, thankfully, there was no sign of any buildup on the airframe. He was nearing the last turning point for the final leg of the flight. There was very little forward view, and he really had no idea if he was on track or not; he was flying on instruments alone with no visual reference to terrain features. *Ah well, just fly the flight plan and go by dead reckoning; that's all one can do*, he thought. Checking the time by his wristwatch, he turned onto the new heading with the fervent hope that something would begin to show soon, as they were just at the border crossing point.

As he flew along, he realized that, having just shot a man for the first time in his life, he felt no reaction, no remorse, no pity, just a real sense of relief that it wasn't himself who was dead. *Well*, he mused to himself, *at least there's been no airborne activity from the "ungodly" tonight. Probably don't want to get wet! Can't say I blame them. I can think of a lot of other things I'd rather be doing at the moment! I'll just flog on and see where we end up.* He then mentally went over his options. *If I did reach the end of my flight plan and could see nothing, what to do? There's no radio on board, so there's no way they could triangulate me; even if I could communicate with air traffic, there's no way they could spot me on radar. Oh well, let's just press on and play it off the cuff. Nothing more I can do!*

As he passed over the border, the rain abated somewhat, and the clouds seemed to be lifting; then a glimmer of luminescence up ahead, some sort of lights. Then he saw, just ahead and below him, a distinct water feature intersecting with his course. It was irregular, not a straight line, therefore not a canal but a river, quite a large one, in fact. He was a little off course. It has to be the river Alter that runs through Celle in a northwesterly direction. He turned and followed it. The lights ahead grew in strength, and as he drew nearer, they took on the familiar form of the town itself. Heaving a sigh of relief, he then turned his attention to the landing ahead. First, how was the passenger coping? He'd been very quiet. *Damn it! I hope the poor sod hasn't died on me*, John thought. Then he spoke. "Are you okay, doctor?"

"Yes," came the reply. "As well as might be expected. Are we nearly there? I see some lights up ahead."

"Yes," John answered. "That's the town of Celle, where we shall be landing very soon. By the way, your English is very good. Where did you learn to speak it so well?"

"I took a degree at Cambridge in 1934, as a matter of fact," the passenger replied.

Picking up the familiar railway line and other landmarks, John brought the aircraft gently into the approach. Although the rain was still falling, he could make out the main runway and his grass landing area to the south of it. He carefully selected his point of touchdown. There was a need now to get the machine as close to the entrance to the Bat Hangar as possible so that the crew could heave it into the hangar as quickly as possible. Throttling back a little more to maintain forty knots, he gently touched down on the remaining right wheel with the tail still up. He put in a fair amount of right aileron to hold the left wing up as long as possible and, using rudder, steered the aircraft toward the now-visible gate to the hangar. *Thank God*, he said quietly to himself, *someone has had the good sense to open it!* As it came closer, the airspeed decreased as he gently throttled back, holding up the wing until it was no longer possible, and they passed through the opening, heading for the hangar doors. Johnny felt the left wing dropping as he approached the doors. The left wingtip touched the ground. As it did so, John jammed on the remaining starboard brake as hard as he could and simultaneously cut off the magneto switches, stopping the engine. The aircraft did not swerve left as much as he expected it to, and it ground to a halt about ten feet from the doors. *Bloody lucky*! he thought. Then he heard a groan from his passenger.

As he clambered rapidly out of the cockpit, the ground crew came scrambling out of the office. He shouted to them, "The passenger's injured! He needs help as soon as possible!" He stepped forward, released the doctor's harness, and let down the small flap door. Paddy was alongside first whilst the ground crew stood by with fire extinguishers. "It just so happens I've got an ambulance, complete with a doctor, standing by. Thought we might need one, just in case! We'll have him downtown in a jiffy once we get him out of here." The doctor came forward and checked his patient, and then after a few words, lifted the passenger's arm and gave him an injection.

"Right then, let's get him out of there and on his way," the doctor ordered.

As the ambulance sped away, Ginger piped up with, "I see Biggles Esquire has gone and buggered up the machinery again!" John, laughing, retorted with, "If you made sure the bloody nuts and bolts were done up properly, I wouldn't have to land this way so often!" Leaving the crew to wrestle with the remains, Paddy and John went into the office to debrief. At the end of it, Paddy said, "It couldn't have been much fun, but by heavens you did it. Those sods were probably the local STASI. Don't worry about shooting the bastard; they're mostly ex-Nazi Gestapo thugs and are hated by the local population. Thank God you took the precautions you did. In these sorts of situations, always shoot first and ask questions after! I'll make sure the powers-to-be understand what a great job you did. Anyway, let's get you downtown for a drink and a bite to eat, and then get you on your way to Sylt."

SIXTEEN

The squadron at Sylt progressed through the month as usual with minor glitches for weather. The Friesian Islands in January are not a terribly hospitable locale. For John, the task of being the gunnery officer for the squadron was absorbing. The process of checking all the gun sight cine film and analysing that against the actual scores achieved on the target banners was very rewarding. The scores of the individuals were as avidly analysed by the pilots as any competitive event anywhere. By analysing the film, pilots could be shown where they were making mistakes. Of course, the competition for the best scores was intense, but, also, the larger event was the results compared with other squadrons. Intersquadron rivalry was intense.

To assist with all this, he also went up for a trip as the observer in the target towing Mosquito to see exactly how the attacks looked from the target's viewpoint. The curves of pursuit could be assessed, and the attack pilots could be properly debriefed after the event. The target banners were rectangular canvas material, five feet high and twenty-five feet long. They were attached to a steel pole spreader bar, weighted with a heavy metal ball at the base to stabilise the banner and allow it to fly upright on its three-hundred-yard-long towline. Each of the four attacking aircraft had their ball ammunition tipped with a different colour paint that left a coloured hole if it passed through the fabric of the banner. Each aircraft carried only one hundred rounds;

therefore, the number of hits physically recorded could be expressed as a percentage.

Having flown the one trip as an observer, John immediately approached the flight commander of the target towing squadron and suggested that if he were to be given a checkout on the "Mossie" he could help them out by standing in from time to time for one of their hard-worked pilots. Additionally, he could check his own people at the same time. The flight commander enthusiastically embraced this idea, and John was able to fly this fascinating and very historic aircraft. The de Havilland Mosquito was aptly named the "Wooden Wonder," and it earned a huge reputation during the war from people on all sides of the conflict. To the observer, it was a sleek and elegant machine in the de Havilland tradition, yet it somehow imparted an impression of rugged strength. Its adaptability was impressive, and, as a result, it had been utilised in many differing roles. Although the Mossie was now obsolete, the Mark 35 target-towing version had been developed from the Mark 6 bomber, which had been modified with a larger bomb bay in order to carry a four thousand pound bomb. The unit also had a Mark 3 trainer version with dual controls used for converting pilots and for flight checks. After absorbing the pilots notes for the aircraft and a very thorough briefing, John completed his checkout flight and went for his first solo run immediately afterward.

The Mosquito, like most de Havilland aircraft, was a sensitive machine. It was a delight to handle and had a formidable performance. It also required sensitive hands to fly it properly and could be very unforgiving if mishandled. Sitting to the left in the tight two-seat cockpit with the empty navigator or observer's seat set back to the right, there was a good view forward over the nose. The two close-set Rolls Royce Merlin MK 113 engines sat level with the cockpit, each capable of 1690 hp at 3,000 rpm plus eighteen pounds of boost from the two-speed single stage superchargers. The throttle movement was very sensitive and needed to be handled very carefully at takeoff. The boost for takeoff was plus two pounds at first, and then gently opening up to a max of plus twelve pounds only after the rudder became effective. Any great imbalance between the two could result in a rather vicious swing.

John opened the throttles gingerly, checking the gauges carefully before releasing the brakes. The Mossie accelerated quite swiftly. Feeling the rudders bite at about forty knots, he eased the throttles open smoothly with a very thrilling roar as all twenty-four cylinders of the two superb V12 engines bellowed out their unmistakable song. The tail came up almost automatically, and, keeping straight with a touch of left rudder, the speed built rapidly. At about 110 knots, the Mossie wanted to fly. A caress of backward pressure on the control column, and she lifted smoothly off the ground. With a positive rate of climb established, he accelerated to the single engine safety speed of 148 knots, retracting the undercarriage, which came up slowly, maintaining 155 knots until the red indicator lights were out. With the drag removed, the Mossie became a very sleek airframe, and now it accelerated like a cat off hot bricks. It was in its element, and so was John.

The jets he had flown were very smooth and fast, more so than the Mossie, but what they lacked was the pure animal feeling of a high-powered, piston-driven aircraft. The sound and the fury, all the little vibrations, the total pulsing explosive energy, was intoxicating. It was the difference between driving a smooth, sophisticated limousine and a supercharged 4½ litre Bentley open sports car, when every nuance of performance becomes a tactile thing. A machine not to be tamed but persuaded to give out its utmost, as a spirited stallion will gallop and run till it drops.

For the next forty-five minutes, he explored the envelope of the aircraft's performance—loops, rolls, wingovers, chandelles and Derry turns. Everything but snap roll manoeuvres and spins; not kind things to do to a beautiful aircraft, unless dire necessity called. The unique wooden structure of the Mosquito gave John a unique feeling. It was as though the plywood/balsa/plywood sandwich sectioned monocoque fuselage was like the sound box of a violin, and the multilayered main wing spar was like a longbow. Tiny vibrations were like notes of music, and to fly it was to play a concerto on a Stradivarius. To John, this day, another wonderful flying experience had happened, and as he cruised smoothly and serenely back to the airfield, he felt he had become one with the aircraft, and it had become an extension of himself.

He entered the downwind leg of the circuit, gradually reducing speed to 130 knots, lowering the undercarriage, down and locked, three green lights, mixture to rich, pitch to 2,600 rpm, and then the flap to thirty degrees, radiator shutters to open. With everything "down and dirty," the drag increased significantly, so a little added power to maintain the speed through the turn onto final approach, in a gradual descent rolling out on the runway heading. Full flap now, elevator trim to compensate, remember to check the flap lever back to neutral, check three green lights again, a little more power to correct any tendency to undershoot, then, with everything in place, cross the threshold at 110 knots, a gentle back pressure on the control column, fly it softly onto the runway on the main wheels, gently throttling back as the wheels whisper their arrival on the tarmac surface, the speed decays, the tail sinks softly onto the deck, use plenty of rudder to keep straight but don't overcorrect, a sense of the beginning of a swing, counteract with a caress on the brake lever and rudder, speed well down now, and we are firmly on the ground. Taxi clear of the runway, flaps up, and after landing checks complete, John felt a warm glow of contentment as he taxied back to dispersal, and he thought, *Surely, this has to be the most wonderful job in the world!*

After shutdown and signing the form 700 in the flight office, John sought out the flight commander and thanked him profusely. "Any time you need me I'd be very happy to fly a tow for you when the squadron is not on the range, and the boss can spare me," he said, meaning every word. "I'll certainly take you up on that!" came the reply.

The month detachment passed in a heartbeat, or so it felt to John. Back at Celle, the squadron settled back into its normal routine and a week had passed. The boss called John into his office. "Johnny, something has come in that's right up your street; I think you'd be very interested."

"Oh, what's that, sir?"

"Well, it's a seminar that's to be held at Farnborough to decide upon a standardized cockpit design and layout for future fighters. You're always vocal on the subject, so how about it?"

"That sounds great, boss. I'd love to do it. When is it going to take place?"

"Okay, Johnny, you have to be there for Sunday the twenty-first, and the seminar starts on the Monday morning. It will last for two weeks."

"I've just thought, sir, there's a couple of things happening at home at the beginning of May. I'd very much like to be there to attend. Any chance I could have a couple of weeks leave to follow?"

"I don't see why not. Sure, go and see the adj and I'll sign it off. Let's see, that should put you back here by the twenty-first of March, I think. Right?"

"Yes, sir, and thank you."

Later that evening, John saw Paddy in the bar and mentioned the seminar. Paddy mused for a moment and said, "Good, there are a couple of things you could do whilst you're over there. I'll see if we can't fix you up with a ride home. We'd best have a chat before you go."

A couple of days passed, and the wing commander flying spotted John in the bar and mentioned that he'd heard John was going on the seminar and how he would like to hear the results when John returned. "By the way," he added, "there's a Lincoln from Upwood flying in here on Thursday the eighteenth. I'll ask the pilot if he could give you a ride back to UK if you'd like me to." John's spirits leapt at the opportunity. "That would really be marvelous, sir; thank you very much indeed. I'll be ready and waiting." After his recent checkout in the Mosquito, he'd thought about what it must have been like to fly something like the Lancaster, with four Merlins, particularly as he had recently flown down over the Mohne Dam whilst doing an air test on one of the Vampires. He had flown the same pattern as the "Dam Busters" had followed on their famous attack and thought, in wonder, as he flew it, *Hell, it must have been a hairy job in a big aircraft.*

On the Thursday afternoon, the Lincoln arrived, and John was ready and waiting. The aircraft taxied onto the parking area by the control tower, and he went out to meet it. The door in the right rear fuselage opened, and a crew member lowered a short ladder to the ground, engines still running at tickover. John handed up his two small bags and climbed aboard; the Lincoln started to taxi at once. The crew member stowed the two bags and led him forward up the fuselage, pointing out the Elsan toilet at the rear of the entrance door, then past an assortment of mysterious-looking photographic and other equipment, up to the main wing spar box, with a rest bunk on the left. Over the spar, the radio operator, sitting on the left at his station, nodded to John; then in front of him, again on the left, sat the navigator under the greenhouse canopy. Ahead of him was the pilot, and, to his right, the flight engineer standing in a passageway that led down to the nose compartment. He handed John a spare headset and showed him where to plug it in. Now on intercom, the pilot said, "Welcome aboard. We'll get underway now. Get you settled down later."

During the climb out, John stood behind the engineer, who was now seated on a hinge-down seat, listening to all the litany of checklists and observing the array of engine instruments and layout of the controls. They levelled off at sixteen thousand feet; the pilot engaged the autopilot and trimmed off the engines to cruise settings, adjusting the propellor pitch and throttles to synchronise the engines. The four great Rolls Royce Merlin 68 engines, rated at 1,750 hp, built by Packard under licence, driving de Havilland Hydramatic propellers, smoothly easing along in cruise at 2,650 rpm and plus seven pounds of boost, put out their unmistakable sibilant roar. John was reminded of his recent experience with the Mosquito, and, for all the difference in airframe, the engine operation and handling was virtually identical. He mused that a transition would be a simple matter.

The pilot noticed his attention to all of the details and enquired, "Ever flown one of these?"

"No, but I did check out on the Mossie a month ago."

"Did you now! Well, you shouldn't have any trouble with this, then. How would you like to sit here a while and look after the shop while I nip down the back and take a snooze for a couple of hours? We'll leave Bob here, the engineer, to look after you for a while. He can answer any questions you might have. Okay?"

The engineer stood up and folded up his seat, and the pilot slid off his seat with practiced ease, showed John where to plug in his headset, and disappeared to the rear of the aircraft. John slid onto his seat; the engineer showed him the seat adjustment, and he settled in comfortably to take stock of his new surroundings. After the cramped confines of the Mosquito and the Vampire, the Lincoln felt enormous. One sat high in the extensive glazed canopy with a good view all around and downward on the left between the port number two engine and the fuselage and over the foreshortened nose. The controls were well placed, and one could clearly see the main flying instruments on the standard RAF panel. The throttles felt very comfortable, and fitted to the right hand perfectly. There, on the centre pedestal, were the pitch and mixture controls, where they could be easily manipulated by either the pilot or the engineer. It was all very straightforward and sensible, and, once one became accustomed to the multiplicity of engine instruments, very simple.

"What do you think, then?" Bob, the engineer, inquired.

"I like it," came the reply from John.

"Do you want to hand fly it for a while to get the feel of it?"

"That would be super. I'll try not to rock the boat too much." John then pressed the autopilot cutout button on the control wheel and felt the aircraft come alive in his hands. It was well trimmed for level flight and felt quite stable. He tried a gentle turn port then smoothly rolled back into a turn starboard, then back again onto the original heading. "Hope that didn't foul you up too much, navigator!" he said over the intercom.

"Not at all; didn't feel a thing," came the reply. "Actually, we do need a new heading, if you'd like to turn onto two nine eight now, that would be great!"

Settling down on the new heading, John assessed the feel of the whole machine. It was not as heavy to fly as he had imagined; it responded well and positively, with no drama or instability whatsoever. *No wonder it, and the Lancaster before it, have the reputation they have,* he thought to himself.

As darkness fell, they droned on into the night, and he mused over the development of the two aircraft. The Lancaster was an astounding success story. The two other British heavy bombers of World War II, the Stirling and the Halifax, never achieved the feats of load carrying achieved by the Lancaster. Its large bomb bay carried a normal load of around fourteen thousand pounds. However, it could also carry the twelve thousand pound "Tallboy" bomb. Ultimately, it would carry the enormous twenty-two thousand pound "Grand Slam" bomb, designed to penetrate very thick concrete then create an earthquake effect below. This was the largest bomb carried by any air force in that war. The aircraft was also unusual in that its performance exceeded the predictions of its chief designer, Roger Chadwick of A. V. Roe. He was hard pressed to explain the phenomenon but surmised it was probably because of the low-slung engines, whose nacelles left all the top part of the wing leading edge exposed to the full slipstream effect from the engines, inducing greater lift than would occur with normal, higher, nacelle placement, which tends to blank off the lift effect behind it. In 1943, there was a requirement for greater range and altitude, and this led to the development of the Lancaster by extending its wingspan to 120 feet and installing the up-rated Merlins. At the same time, the fuselage was extended by some ten feet, along with a strengthened undercarriage and heavier-calibre guns. At first this was simply called the Lancaster Mk 4, but, in light of all the extensive changes, the new aircraft was renamed "Lincoln." The beauty of it was that crews required very little conversion training because, except for the numbers, it was essentially the same to fly as the Lancaster.

They flew west over Holland and the North Sea. Approaching the coast of England, the pilot came forward. John relinquished control, and then stood, watched, and listened with interest to the intercom and the approach to RAF Upwood, where they were to land. He was impressed with the cool efficiency and lack of drama on the part of the crew. No unnecessary idle chatter, just sheer professionalism that was a joy to behold. Then they were on final approach, with the runway lights ahead. The touchdown was in the tail down attitude and was smooth with no drama. As they taxied in the pilot said, "By the way, my name is George. Sorry, I should have said so earlier. I understand you're trying to get over to Wymeswold tomorrow?"

"That's right."

"Well I've been thinking. I have an air test to do tomorrow. What we could do is drop you off there quite easily."

"That would be marvelous," John enthused. "What time's the air test?"

"Well, I was planning a bit of a 'lie-in' in the morning. How does briefing at nine and takeoff at ten sound? We can buzz about a bit then drop you off at, er, say twelve or so, okay?"

"Thanks very much. I'm looking forward to it all."

Next morning, after the briefing, which was simply a check on the weather, which was forecast to be cool and clear, sunny with a light breeze, they drove over to the hangar, outside which the ground crew were readying the Lincoln. After parking the Land Rover, George and John walked over to the aircraft and met the flight engineer, who was completing his external preflight checks. "Morning, Skipper! It all seems to be in one piece!"

"Well that's a blessing. Has the chiefy got the 700?"

"Yes, he's walking out with it now; says she's all ready to go."

After checking the form, George thanked the flight sergeant, and he and John commenced the captain's external, walk-around check, pointing out the salient items that every pilot needs to check before any flight. As they climbed aboard the aircraft, they moved forward, George pointing out some internal items on the way. Reaching the cockpit area, George remarked, "You'll notice this one is set up as a trainer and has a set of controls in the engineer's position. Why don't you jump into the left-hand seat and fly it? I'll sit and watch. Actually, I'm the squadron check pilot, so it will be quite legal."

"Super. That would be marvellous, I really did enjoy the bit of flying I did on the way over last night. It's a great aircraft!"

"Well, I hope you don't find it too dull after the Mossie."

They ran the checklists and started the engines one at a time, commencing with the starboard inner, number three. The engine start procedure was the same as for the Merlins on the Mosquito. All four settled down to an even cackle, then run up to max rpm, against the chocks, check pressures and temperatures all okay. Throttle back, accompanied by the customary crackle and pops. Run the pretaxi checks, call for taxi clearance. Wave the chocks away, release the brakes; the aircraft starts to roll forward. Dab on the brake lever; that checks the brakes. George reminds John, "Remember, to change direction, just give the opposite outboard engine a touch of power using a touch of power, then back off early before she swings too far. Don't forget that when we're light, as we are now with no load on board, she'll accelerate quite rapidly so you'll have to use a dab or two of brake to hold the speed down."

After a couple of trial swings to port and starboard, checking the flight instruments for full function, John caught the hang of it, and they taxied along to the takeoff point without any drama. The pretakeoff checks were run, and they called for takeoff clearance. Lining up on the centre line of the runway, John paused for a moment to take in the view forward. He had been used to sitting only a few feet off the runway in all the previous aircraft he had flown. Now he was sitting more than twenty feet up, and this gave a very different aspect of the runway; suddenly, the Lincoln seemed to be a very large aircraft, and the runway seemed narrower than normal. "It seems a long way off the ground," he remarked to George. "I suppose it does. Don't worry about it; everyone feels that way at first. After a couple of takeoffs and landings it will all seem quite normal," George replied.

John ran the engines up, checking the revs and pressures with a glance, released the brakes, right hand on the four throttles with the thumb advancing the port outer engine to correct any incipient swing, accelerating now, stick forward to bring the tail up, touch of rudder to keep her straight. Glance down at the airspeed indicator, passing eighty-five knots, she wants to fly, a gentle backpressure on the control wheel, the cushioned bumping of the large balloon tires fades away and that great wing lifts the Lincoln into its natural element. Positive rate of climb, dab on the brake lever to stop the wheel rotation, select undercarriage up, accelerating now to climb speed, flaps up. After-takeoff checklist follows. Power set at 2,650 rpm and plus four pounds boost, they climb away.

For the next hour, George led John through a series of exercises—feathering props, shutting down and restarting engines, double asymmetric handling (two engines feathered on the same side), a series of stalls, tight turns followed by some exaggerated wingovers, and other, near aerobatic, manoeuvres. With growing confidence, John felt his way with this remarkable aircraft. It seemed to do everything well. Easy to fly, responsive to the controls, yet docile. Quite forgiving with absolutely no vices, it could almost be said a dull aircraft to fly. Yet, it was not! It would certainly reward a good pilot and would endear itself to the degree that, having flown one, a pilot would never ever forget the experience.

They had worked their way toward Wymeswold, and George intimated, "I think we should try a few landings now." They called the tower at Wymeswold for permission to carry out a few touch-and-go landings and descended to circuit height. As they approached the airfield, George said, "I'll talk you through the first one and see how we go. I don't think you'll have any problem at all. It's actually easier to land than a Mossie. Just aim to touch down a little farther down the runway than you normally do, and you'll find it all works out."

At the end of the downwind leg, before-landing checklist complete, John turned crosswind when it felt right, a little further on than normal. Then, with wheels down and locked, with three green lights, and one notch of flap, reducing power a little, commenced a descending turn onto final approach. John had set the seat adjusted up high, which gave a clear view over the nose, and the cockpit side was down at waist level. In combination with the many-windowed canopy, it gave an excellent field of view all round. Rolling out of the turn onto the runway heading, still descending at a steady rate, John, concentrating on a touchdown point about a third of the way down the runway, lowered landing flap and adjusted the elevator trim. Holding the same attitude and descent rate, the speed decreased to 105 knots. "That's about right for a normal approach," George encouraged. "Maintain this and go for a wheeler landing, first of all. As you round out, throttle back gently or else it'll float on forever!"

John followed the suggestion, and, with a slight bounce, the Lincoln touched down without any drama. As the speed decayed, he allowed the tail to settle gently down. At the end of the runway, they turned onto the peritrack and taxied back to the takeoff point. Then followed another takeoff, followed by several touch-and-go landings, including a double asymmetric one with no flap, which entails a longer, flatter approach at higher than normal landing speeds. With each one, John became more comfortable, and for the final landing he simply carried out a three-pointer, which felt right. It all worked beautifully, and he relished the thought of flying the aircraft again. As they taxied to the hangar where the ground crew awaited them, George remarked, "That was a nice session. You don't seem to have any problems with the aircraft. Anytime you feel you'd like to take a trip or put in a bit of continuation practice, just let me know, and I'd be glad to fit you in, okay?"

"That I would like to do, when I get the opportunity. Thanks a lot for this ride over here today and for your time and trouble running me through the programme. It really was very kind of you," John enthused.

"Not at all, old lad. I do mean what I say. If you ever think of coming to Bomber Command, just let me know. We really could use you!"

Twenty minutes later, John was on the Vincent and heading for home for the weekend before heading for Farnborough on Sunday morning. As he passed through Ashby, he spotted a car he knew parked outside The Bull in Market Street. Known as the oldest pub in Ashby-de-la-zouch, it sits halfway down the wide street, where an annual fare is held, "The Ashby Statutes." The pub was frequented by his closest friend, Eric, and, of course, his mentor, Harry. It was Harry's car he had seen, so he stopped, parked the Vincent, and went in. Thus began a splendid short weekend in his home territory amongst his nearest and dearest friends and their families.

SEVENTEEN

Walking into the mess bar at Farnborough on Sunday evening, John found half a dozen old friends and acquaintances. Some had come in from overseas commands, others from Fighter Command in the United Kingdom; he seemed to be the only one from Second TAF in Germany. One thing they all had in common was that they were all high scorers in armament delivery, and several of them were currently on aerobatic teams. It could be assumed that they were all rising stars, also that they had egos to match! The old RAF saying flashed through his mind, *"Whipped in with the cream and came out a clot!"* *Ah! Well, we'll see,* he thought, *this should be a very interesting week.*

By the end of the evening, all twelve members of the panel had arrived, and a considerable party had developed. They were a convivial bunch of characters with an endless supply of stories and tales to tell, and, in the traditional manner, the booze flowed freely. As the evening progressed, John noticed an officer who quietly slipped into the bar unnoticed by the rest of the crowd. He stood quietly by the bar sipping on half a pint of bitter, unobtrusively scanning the assembled crowd. His eyes met with John's and moved on, but an instant flash of recognition registered with them both. He was a member of the staff from the country house establishment where John would be reporting for further instruction following his departure from Farnborough.

The following morning, they assembled in a particular building and were all standing around a cockpit mock-up peering into it and speculating wildly. They were brought to attention by the presence of a wing commander who entered the room.

"Good morning, gentlemen," he began by way of greeting. "Do have a seat, and I'll tell you what this seminar is all about." He went on to explain there was a great diversity in past and existing fighter cockpits. Various controls were scattered haphazardly about, as were many switches and gauges. There were even differences between marks of the same aircraft. This created a dangerous situation when one began to consider the discharge of armament. Indeed, many accidental happenings of this nature were occurring, to the danger of life and limb of local populations. Every incident investigation pointed toward this being a common factor. The situation had begun because the designers and engineers tended to position the items where there was a handy space available. Chief test pilots, who accepted the initial designs, grew accustomed to the distribution and rarely commented on them.

The great redeeming feature of the RAF was its standardised basic flying panel, used on every type of aircraft. Here, the six major instruments required for instrument flying were neatly and logically grouped together on one panel, placed high and central to all others, ensuring that a pilot never had to look for those essential items, no matter what aircraft he flew, without having to scan a great variety of nonessential information. This was a great safety factor that other air forces and civil airlines were just beginning to appreciate.

The object of this seminar was to extend this principle to all single-seat fighter aircraft controls. The wing commander went on to point out the cockpit mock-up. It was fitted with the latest Martin Baker ejection seat, flanked by horizontal sloping metal panels on each side, the left-hand one having a throttle lever mounted in the normal position. Bridging the two side panels, filling the cross section of the fuselage in front of the pilot, was a further slightly sloping vertical panel, upon which was superimposed the standard flying panel. On a side table were a collection of all the levers, knobs, switches, and gauges required for a fighter aircraft and for management of its armament and other systems. These were all magnetized and could be placed anywhere on the metal panels. The group of pilots was there to come to an agreed position for all of these items, thus creating a standardised layout.

At ten thirty, there was a break for coffee, and the wing commander joined in with the group and answered many of the questions they had. As they reassembled to begin work, he reminded them all that what they were doing, and the conclusions they came to, was highly classified and subject to the Official Secrets Act. Later, during the lunch break, John went to his room and found a note lying on his dressing table. It was from George, telling him that the instructor from the school was there to liase with him and he should meet with him casually that evening in a local pub for a briefing.

Later that evening, John was standing at the cosy little bar, sipping a pint of bitter in the lounge. He was the sole customer. A person entered whom he recognized at once from his previous visits to the Manor. After the usual casual greetings, they moved from the bar to a quiet corner table, where they would not be overheard. Bill opened the conversation. "Well, how's the seminar going so far?"

John took a sip of his drink and replied, "I think we're all wasting our time. Every one of us has our own idea of how things should be. We all agree that the present system is chaotic and that the only sensible thing is the standard flying panel we have at present. We also all agree that the rest of the bits and pieces should also have a standard presentation laid out in a logical fashion. Personally, I think we will never reach any firm conclusion, and the best thing to do is to hand the problem over to an expert in logic, and let him sort it out. After he produces a solution, then get a couple of us to look at it and see if we have any great quarrel with it. After that, everyone would quickly get comfortable with it, just like the basic instrument panel."

After a pause to reflect, Bill said, "That sounds like a sensible idea to me; of course, I'm not a pilot, but it seems the way to go. Look, I have an idea. Why don't you approach the bloke in charge and suggest that to him? Then see what he comes up with. My feeling is that he will most probably agree with you and get one of his staff to work on the problem. Now! That's going to take a few days to come up with the goods, and that would leave you some free time. We really need you down at the Manor whilst you're here, so if you could persuade him to let you off the hook, you could spend some time with us. What do you think?"

"I think that's a great idea. I'll see the wingco first thing."

The next morning, after the group had assembled, the wing commander left the room for his office, followed by John. As they walked along the passage, John enquired, "May I have a word in private, sir?" They moved into the office and the wing commander gestured to a chair. "Make yourself comfortable and tell me what's on your mind." John briefly explained his feelings about their efforts so far and went on to frame out the suggested proposal. After a brief pause, the wing commander smiled wryly at John and said, "That bears out my feelings about the problem; we've been down this road already, and I reached just about the same conclusion. Now I'll let you in on a secret. We already have one of our chaps beavering away on it. I daresay he'll come up with an answer soon. When he does, we'll throw the result at your lot and see what you think of it, okay?"

"Well, if that's the case, sir, is there a chance I could clear off for a few days? I've some leave coming up, and I'm not due back at Celle until March 21."

"That sounds like a good idea, John. I'll make your excuses for you, and you can take off right away. By the way, thanks very much for your input; it certainly sounds like common sense to me. I'll contact your boss and tell him, so also thank him for sending over someone with a bit of practical sense."

John reported to the Manor that evening and began some very intensive training in self-defence, unarmed combat, weapons, and communication codes. During the course of one of the unarmed combat sessions, one of the countless pieces of advice given by the instructor was, "If you are going to attack someone, try to distract them by looking harmless; then, hit them very suddenly without signalling your move, very hard in a vital spot, and then instantly follow up with a couple more very hard blows to cripple them. Don't pause for an instant." He followed this advice with a detailed description of spots on the body where nerve centres are located. John listened very attentively to this briefing and then asked for it to be repeated, sensing its vital importance. Something told him that this could possibly save his life at some future point. Another interesting point was, when not in uniform try to blend in with the public—lose the military bearing, slouch a bit, round the shoulders, and look down. Walk at a steady pace and don't swing the arms. Any sort of smartness is a dead giveaway! Don't look over your shoulder to see if someone is following; instead, glance in shop windows for reflections or stop and cross the road, using that as a reason to look around, and so on. The whole object is to blend into the surroundings without being obvious about it.

Briefing followed briefing, and more lectures, drills, and exercises. A week passed quickly by. A short leave followed before John returned to Germany.

EIGHTEEN

March 19, 1954.

It was a Friday; John had been back from United Kingdom for a couple of weeks now and settled comfortably into the normal squadron life. There had been a fair amount of chat recently about the ever-expanding NATO coordination, and several joint exercises with other armed forces had taken place in the last few months. None was of any great significance, as far as the squadron was concerned. However, speculation was rife of new activity. When John strolled into the Keller Bar that evening, he saw the new squadron adjutant, Mike, chatting to Norman, his flight commander. Seeing John, Norman beckoned him over, bought him a drink, and said, "Mike here tells me that a message came in late this afternoon that may involve us."

"Oh, really, what's it all about then?" John queried.

"Have you ever heard of a TWETS?" chipped in Mike.

"Can't say I have. Is it some sort of curious sex act?" came the reply.

"No, you idiot," Mike retorted, "Its jargon for 'Tactical Exercise Without Troops.' It sounds very much like something the Pongos have dreamt up. Anyway, it would seem that we are likely to be involved in it. The boss is going to brief us all on Monday morning."

At the Monday normal daily briefing, the boss went into some detail of the setup and the international composition of the personnel who would be taking part. The British contingent would have three RAF

119

officers, three army and three navy, in order to have a representative from each service on duty around the clock. The other nations would have a similar representation. He explained that the operating language would be English, and a standard message format would be employed for the signals traffic. The rest of the details would be announced at the comprehensive briefing to be given at the start of the exercise itself, which was to take place in the British army barracks in Essen. He went on to say only one officer was going from the squadron, who would be nominated later. Later that day, the boss saw John in the crew room and asked him to step into his office for a moment. Inside he said, "Well, Johnny, it seems you are the chosen one to go on this TWETS affair. You go down there by train on Thursday."

On the way to Essen by train, the door to John's compartment opened, and he was joined by Paddy, dressed in civilian clothes, who said, "What ho, sport, mind if I sit a while? I see you're all alone in here. Perhaps we could have a chat about the week ahead." "Why, certainly," John replied. "Are there things I should know about?"

"Yes, indeed. As you know already, this is a joint effort involving all our 'allies,' and it is all about our communications. We believe there will be those attending who do not necessarily have our best interests at heart. Sad to say, but we know there may be one or two whom we suspect of having a direct link to 'Uncle Joe' from the opposition."

"Well, do we know who they are?"

"Not really. We suspect the French or Belgians might have a mole, but we can't pin anyone in particular. That's where you come in. All our intelligence people are known to the opposition, but they don't know about you. As far as they are concerned, you're just a run-of-the mill pilot, along with all the others on this exercise."

"Okay. Exactly what do you need me to do?" queried John.

"First of all, keep a low profile; try not to draw undue attention to yourself. Just keep your eyes and ears open, and observe everybody there. Certainly our previously mentioned 'Amis.' Should you see anything suspicious or untoward, don't raise any alarms; we need to follow the trail and see where it leads us. I'll give you a local phone number where you can contact me on the 'QT.' Don't call unless there's something positive. Okay?" With that, he handed John a note with the telephone number on it and left the compartment. John looked at the number, memorized it, and then tore the note into pieces, and, opening the compartment window, let the scraps of paper blow away in the slipstream.

Later, after arriving at the army mess, checking in, and having dinner, he paid a visit to the bar. It was filled with officers from many countries, and he looked around for a familiar face. He only saw one other RAF officer, another pilot. After getting a gin and tonic, John went over to him and said, "Hello I'm Johnny Ferguson from Celle." "Tommy Thompson from Wildenrath," came the reply. They chatted for a while in a casual way before leaving the bar to turn in for the night.

The following morning they met again at a briefing held in the room where the exercise was to be run and were joined by a third RAF officer, a navigator from the headquarters at Buckeberg. After introducing themselves to each other, John remarked, "Looks as though we're it for the RAF." At that point, the briefing began. The briefing officer was an army major of the signals corps, who proceeded to explain the way the operation was to be run in shifts and then went into the details of how the signals were to be handled. The scenario was that the Soviets, during their annual exercises close to the Iron Curtain, had suddenly begun an aggressive move across the line. Our reaction and response to the threat would be the object of the exercise.

As the briefing proceeded with the details given by several other officers, John, who had sat near the rear and to one side of the room, took a gentle look around to observe the others. Some were showing signs of boredom, a couple nodding off to sleep. One or two were taking notes, and John looked a little more closely at them. One was a young American officer complete with crew cut hair; John sensed that he was probably "gung ho" and very earnest. Another was a Dutch pilot who appeared to have difficulty understanding what was being said. The third one was a French officer who had maintained a rather supercilious expression on his face from the moment he entered the room but now appeared to be paying rapt attention to every detail and was scribbling down every point. *Worth keeping an eye on this chappie,* thought John. *Let's see what he gets up to.'*

The day dragged on in a flurry of paperwork; lunch was bought in, and at 1700 hours, shift change took place. Almost to a man, they headed off to the officers mess bar for another bout of socialising. John kept an eye open for the Frenchman, who seemed to hover around a small group of people. He introduced himself as "Marcel" and then hovered, listening, but contributing nothing before moving on to another group. After half an hour or so he left the bar, and John quietly followed. The Frenchman went to the telephone booth situated in the mess entrance hall, made a call, which was very brief, and then went to his room. Ten minutes or so later he came out and went back to the mess entrance hall. A few minutes later, a taxi drew up outside; the Frenchman got in, and the cab left. John looked hard at the number plate, took out a pencil and jotted the number down inside a book of matches, went back inside, and called Paddy's number. Paddy came on the line. "Paddy," John began, "a subject of interest has just left the mess here in a Mercedes diesel taxi. I would dearly like to know where he went to; here's the cab licence plate number." Paddy read back the number, and then replied, "Stay there a few minutes, and I'll call you back with the info. Let me know if there is anything else you need," and then rang off. Two or three minutes later, Paddy called back with the name of a so-called nightclub, which was, in fact, a somewhat disreputable but quite well-known bar. John thanked him for the information and said that he'd follow up with any developments.

A short while later, he made a collect call to Michelle, who immediately accepted the call. John apologized for not having been in touch for a while, mentioned where he was, and then asked if they could perhaps have dinner together somewhere in Essen one evening in the week. Michelle replied that she'd very much like to do that and added that "Daddy" had an apartment he kept in Essen, which he used during his frequent visits to various interests he had there. They then made a date for two nights ahead. Having exchanged a few pleasantries, Michelle said, "John, you sound as if there's something else. Can you tell me what it is?"

"It must be your feminine intuition, "John replied. "Do you happen to have any contacts of your group here in town?"

"Oh yes! I have two or three there, who I trust very much. We used to work together as a team within our group. I'm sure they will help in any way they can."

"That's marvelous. This is what I could use some help with. I want a person followed discreetly, and I can't allow myself to be detected doing so. I'm sure you'll appreciate why." He went on to explain the situation and how he would like it handled.

The next evening, John received a call from Michelle, who said that she had some information for him, but it would cost him the price of dinner together when they next met. Essentially, the "subject" had been followed to a bar that catered to homosexuals. Inside he had joined a person at a table, where he had passed over a large envelope to that person. He then went to the bar and ordered a drink. The other person had then left the club immediately. The watcher followed that person out of the bar and indicated to the other member of the team to take up the chase. He then returned inside to further observe the Frenchman. The recipient of the envelope then drove off in his car and was discreetly followed to his hotel by the tracker, who happened to be a plainclothes police detective. After a brief wait, the detective spoke to the hotel receptionist and asked for details of the mystery man. He discovered the person's name and the fact that he was a British member of the Control Commission and stayed at the hotel whenever he was in Essen. Having thanked Michelle profusely, John immediately called Paddy and passed on the essential information. Paddy thanked him and asked to meet John the following evening in another nightclub.

John arrived at the appointed place in a taxi and went inside to find Paddy occupying a discreet corner table in an alcove. After a waiter had brought John a beer, Paddy quietly said, "That was a nice piece of work you organized yesterday. Your friend seems to have connections to people in high places."

"She does indeed, seemingly," John countered. "A very useful asset and lovely to boot!"

"Well, her 'info' is as good as her credentials," Paddy went on. "It would seem that our mystery man is somewhat highly placed in the corridors of power in Whitehall. A long-standing, and somewhat senior 'mandarin,' no less! Just what the hell he was doing meeting a serving French officer in a seedy queers bar is a matter of great interest to our masters and powers to be. Ongoing inquires will proceed. 'They' wish you to know that 'they' are pleased with us at our end and send their felicitations!" He tipped his glass in John's direction and drained it, saying, "Now let's have another to celebrate."

NINETEEN

March 29, 1954. Monday.

John had arrived back at Celle from Essen late the night before, and following met briefing, the boss called all the pilots together in the crew room for an announcement.

To the delight of all, he explained that the first of the new Venom aircraft, which were to replace the rather dated and inadequate Vampire Mk 5s the squadron was equipped with, would be arriving that afternoon. This brought forth a great cheer from the assembled pilots, particularly when they were told that these were to be the Mk 2 Venoms, much improved over the Mk 1 version. Later that afternoon, the Venom landed and taxied to the squadron hangar. The ferry pilot climbed out to be greeted by the boss. He explained that he could stay only for an hour or so because another aircraft would be arriving to fly him back to United Kingdom. He was a test pilot from de Havilland and immediately set about briefing the assembled pilots on the Venom, explaining the essential differences vis-à-vis the Vampire, ending his brief with the comment, "I believe you are going to enjoy the experience!"

April 5, 1954. Monday.

A week had passed since the arrival of the first Venom, followed by the arrival of two more. The first one had undergone its statutory ground inspections by the ground crew; the boss had already flown it, and so had the two flight commanders. Today, as gunnery officer for the squadron, it was John's turn to fly it.

As he walked out to the aircraft, he had a strange feeling that something was amiss. Had he forgotten something? Having spent most of the previous evening going carefully through the pilot's notes for the Venom Mk 2, he was confident about most things pertaining, much of it was so similar to the familiar Vampire; no, that wasn't it. His footsteps felt so very light! Then he realized he was only carrying his helmet and oxygen mask. For the first time flying in a jet, he was not humping along a parachute, complete with the accompanying emergency dinghy pack. Again, for the first time, he was going to be sitting on an ejector seat that has all the safety and emergency equipment stowed in it.

He looked down the line of Vampires to the Venom sitting at the end of the row. The most noticeable difference at first glance was the wingtip tanks, permanently fitted to the wing. The wing itself was much slimmer than the Vampire's. The fin and rudder assembly differed also; somehow, the aircraft had a more sinister appearance about it. The big difference was in the engine, which was not visible. De Havilland, besides manufacturing aircraft, also manufactured engines. Their first jet engine, the Goblin, powered the Vampire and produced around 3,350 pounds of thrust. A larger version of the Goblin, named the Ghost, produced a much great thrust of some 5,150 pounds. This engine had been developed to power the world's first jet airliner, the Comet, and it had occurred to some enlightened soul that stuffing one into a Vampire would endow that aircraft with a degree of sparkle it needed to remain competitive. They accompanied that by replacing the Vampire wing with a thinner, more flexible, laminar flow design, allowing a higher Mach number and all-round performance. The centre body of the aircraft was the same as the Vampire, as were the four 20 mm Hispano cannons under the cockpit. The cockpit layout was very similar with the exception of the all-important Martin Baker ejector seat. Also, the old spade grip control column had been replaced by a new pistol grip handle, a small g-meter had been added, and a new, improved compass took the place of the directional gyro heading indicator.

Climbing into the cockpit, he was assisted by a ground crew member, who helped him first strap on the parachute harness and dinghy connection, followed by the seat straps and radio and oxygen connections. Last of all he removed the ejector seat safety pin, attached to a large red disc, showed it to John, and then stowed it in the pocket fitted to the headrest of the seat, and finally gave him a thumbs-up. John took stock of the new "office." The new pistol-grip control column felt just right and far more natural to use. Unlike the old spade grip, it did not obscure the main instrument panel to any great extent, a big improvement! The other great addition was a "relight" capability for the Ghost engine. The old Goblin in the Vampire did not have this incredibly useful device. If the engine "flamed out," the pilot found himself flying a glider, added to which, should he need to bail out of the Vampire, there was a rather complicated procedure to follow that involved inverting the aircraft. The innovation of the ejector seat was a great morale booster, to say the least.

The airman had now walked out well in front of the aircraft and stood waiting for John to start up. The Venom did not use an electric starter motor like the Vampire. Instead, it employed a very large cartridge starter, the same principal as the one John was using on the Bat, but it used a very much larger cartridge in conjunction with a high-energy igniter system. Completing the start-up checklist, he pressed the starter button and was rewarded with a very loud bang, a vast cloud of black smoke, and an engine that was running at idling rpm. *Bloody hell,* he thought to himself, *that was effective.* Completing the rest of the checklists, he taxied out toward the runway. Looking out to each side, the wingtip tanks were quite noticeable, but all else was much the same as the familiar Vampire. Lining up on the runway, he took a quick glance at all the instruments; all was well, and he was cleared for takeoff. On opening the throttle, he was rewarded with a very gratuitous push in the back and splendidly rapid acceleration, takeoff, and subsequent high rate of climb. After the Vampire, this thing climbed like a "homesick angel." As he climbed through the lower turbulent levels, the somewhat bumpy ride experienced in the stiff winged Vampire was replaced with a far more comfortable cushioned ride allowed by the more flexible wing. In fact, looking out at the wingtip tanks, one could see them moving gently up and down as the wing flexed.

Reaching twenty thousand feet, he levelled off and put the aircraft through a series of stalls, in different configurations, to check the responses. Then he followed this up with a session of aerobatics, during which he noted that the aileron control was delightfully more responsive than the Vampire's, but the elevators required more effort. Levelling off after this sequence, he was amazed to find that he had actually gained about fifteen hundred feet. Doing the same sequence in the Vampire, he would have lost some altitude. He also noticed the g-meter readings. He had been pulling four to five g with no untoward effect, other than the normal effort required and the associated feel of heaviness. *Right ho,* he thought, *let's try "greying out" and see how many gs that takes.* He dove the Venom down to quickly gain speed and, at 480 knots, pulled hard into a level steep turn, at the same time opening up to max power to sustain the rate of turn. Now he felt the effort required and did notice the narrowing of vision associated with the greying out, which precedes the "blackout" condition. The partial loss of consciousness experienced began to subside as the high rate of turn decayed. Rolling out of the turn into straight and level flight, he checked the g-meter; the needle that records the maximum g pulled showed seven g. *Well, that's useful to know,* he thought. *In the cold light of day, it's a pretty good number; most people start greying out at four to five g. In a combat situation, with the adrenalin running, I could probably sustain that higher number, and that could be a useful edge.*

Now, he climbed to forty thousand feet, revelling in the greater rate of climb; then, levelling off, he tried a few steep turns. The whole aircraft felt so much more capable than the Vampire had; it was a great confidence booster. Throttling back the engine and then opening the throttle swiftly created no drama. This was something that had to be done gingerly in the Vampire, as it could easily bring on a low temperature flameout in the Goblin engine, and, as that engine had no relight capability, would mean a glide home and an engine out landing. Not only did the Ghost engine in the Venom overcome the flameout propensity, it also had this high-energy relight capability. All of these things were beginning to add up to making the Venom a formidable weapon. Next thing to find out was, how do we evade a MiG 15? Our principle foe, we see them on daily patrols up and down the Curtain, generally above us at forty-three thousand to forty-five thousand feet. Given the fact that they are supposedly capable of exceeding Mach 1.0, what evasive action would he take to get them down to an altitude where the Venom's superior manoeuvrability and acceleration would come into play and offer the possibility of a "kill"? With the Vampire, one's options were somewhat limited, due to the flameout potential and the lack of a powerful air brake. All one could realistically do was to cruise at a lower altitude, where the problems were not so acute. With the Venom, John reasoned, fortified by the relight capability and the blessed addition of the ejector seat, one could manoeuvre with impunity. Quickest way down? *Just let's roll over inverted and pull through into a vertical dive and see what happens,* he thought. Throttling gently back to about one-third power, he rolled into the dive and extended the ineffective air brakes; the Mach number rapidly increased to the limit, at which point he throttled back completely. The ailerons had become very heavy, and the Venom was pitching badly. Trying the elevators for effectiveness proved them to be very heavy and ineffective. The wild ride continued as the aircraft descended rapidly through thirty thousand feet, at which point the Mach number began to decrease to the point where the controls became effective. He levelled out and cancelled the air brake, increasing power to full throttle, and pulled immediately into a very tight climbing turn to regain what he hoped would be a good position to latch onto any imaginary aircraft that might have pursued him through the unusual manoeuvre.

Well, he thought, *not very pretty and probably illegal as far as our lords and masters are concerned, but it's bloody effective to get out of harm's way.* He glanced at the g-meter, which had maximum and minimum recorder needles, and saw that on the recovery he achieved a plus seven and minus two g readings. *Time to try this thing out at low level on my way back to base,* he thought as he entered a maximum-rate descent. Levelling off at five hundred feet, he adjusted the speed to three hundred knots, the normal cruise speed for the Vampire. Once he noticed the much smoother ride the thin wing gave, compared to the Vampire. Looking out at the wingtips again, he could see the tip tanks moving up and down as the wings absorbed the turbulent air at this level. Trying a couple of steep turns, he began to really enjoy the delicate and responsive aileron controls; in fact, the whole aircraft felt just right as he started to analyze its responses. Taking it down to nap-of-the-earth level at about fifty feet and lower, it felt just as comfortable. Confidence rising by the minute, he pushed the speed up to 420 knots and then tried another couple of turns. *This is a great piece of kit,* he mused. *Yes! I'm really going to enjoy this aeroplane; can't wait to try it out against an F86 Sabre from Wildenrath, and it's going to be interesting to see how we do at gunnery scores*. As he rolled out on the landing run some fifty-five minutes after takeoff, he felt a warm glow of satisfaction about the whole trip and the aircraft. Taxing around the perimeter track, back to dispersal in front of the squadron hangar, he thought, *I can't wait to get my machine. I'll zero in the gun sight and bore align the cannon barrels myself, and then take it up to the range and see what sort of a score I can get.*

The next day, the delivery pilots flew in two more Venoms. These were to be allotted to the two flight commanders. The following Monday, one more arrived; this was it! His own aircraft at last! Three days later, just after lunch, the squadron "chiefy" came into the crew room, saw John, went over to him, and said, "Would you like to come and have a look at your aircraft, sir?" He followed the flight sergeant out into the hangar, and there stood the aircraft, resplendent in its factory camouflage finish, the letter D painted on the fuselage nose under the canopy and above it, his rank and name. On each tail boom were painted the squadron markings, a red cross on a white background, and each side of the RAF roundel. "Well, Chiefy, if it flies as well as it looks, it'll be a bit of all right!" John exclaimed.

"It should do," came the reply. "It came through the acceptance check without a snag, and I checked the rigging personally, sir."

"Did you, now? That was very kind of you. Thank you! She's ready for an air test then?"

"Oh yes indeed, sir!" came the reply.

John went straight to the flight commander's office and saw him poring over some paperwork. "Norman, they've got my aircraft glued together, and it's ready for an air test. Do you mind authorizing it for me?"

"Not at all, old boy, glad to oblige. Just don't do anything I wouldn't do!" came the cheery reply. An hour and a half later he was back in the hangar, the test completed, and whilst signing off the maintenance form 700, the chief came over to him and enquired how had the trip gone.

"Perfectly. Not a single snag; it flies like a dream and trims out 'hands off' straight and level, chief. It's just beautiful. Just one thing though. Perhaps, when it's convenient, could we put it up on the gun alignment rig? I would like to harmonize it myself," John said.

"Scheduled for first thing in the morning, sir," came the reply.

That evening, in the Keller Bar, John and Norman were having a drink after dinner. Norman asked John, "How did the air test go with your new toy?"

"Super, thanks. Why do you ask?"

"Well, I thought it was okay after the trip, but I see Chiefy has got it down for another ground check."

"Ah!" exclaimed John. "That's because I asked him to put it up for a harmonization check."

"Oh, why do you want that doing? I thought it had already been done on the acceptance check."

"Glad you asked, Norman. I noticed last time the squadron had an air-to-ground session up on the range, our scores were way below normal. It wasn't anybody in particular. We all were downright awful. There has to be a reason for it, so I'm going to harmonize my own aircraft and see if it makes a difference."

"Well, tomorrow's Friday, and it's our turn on the range, so I daresay we'll find out then. Care for another drink?"

"No thanks, Norman. That's kind of you, but I think I'll turn in for an early night."

Next morning, immediately after the wing briefing, where all three squadrons were briefed on the weather and any other pertinent information, he went directly to the chief's office in the hangar, and after the chief had summoned an armourer, they all went over to his Venom D, perched up on the harmonization rig. The corporal armourer slid the bore scope, a long tube with a lens fitted at right angles near to the end of it, down the barrel of first of the four, 20 mm cannons. He peered down through the lens, looked up at John, and said, "That's it; I think you'll find it's spot on, sir, if you'd care to check it." John looked down through the lens and could see the sighting board on the wall in front of the aircraft. The bore of the cannon was very accurately centred on the proper aiming mark. In turn, the other three barrels were checked and were perfect.

"A very nice job, corporal. Thank you!" John exclaimed.

"Thank you, sir. I did the alignment myself; knew you'd want it done right."

"Okay, now I'll just jump into the cockpit and check the gun sight," said John.

He settled down in the seat, switched on internal electrical power and then the gun sight. The sighting graticules appeared in the reflector glass on top of the sight with the aiming dot in the centre. Looking through the glass, he blinked. The aiming dot was off to the right and below the aiming mark on the sighting board. He switched to the fixed cross mode, and, again, the sighting cross was off to the right and low. Turning his head to the chief, he asked, "Who aligned the sight, Chiefy?"

"Oh, that will be our new instrument man, sir. LAC Dobbs. Shall I get him out here?" Whilst the instrument mechanic was sent for, John asked the chief to hop into the cockpit and look for himself. Doing so, the chief exclaimed, "Good grief, sir, the thing's a mile off!"

A few minutes later, the instrument mechanic appeared and came over to them. He was wearing very thick lens glasses. He saluted smartly and said, "Is everything all right, sir?"

"Did you align this gun sight, Dobbs?" John asked.

"Yes, sir. Is it all right?" came the innocent reply. Not wishing to hurt the young man's feelings, John said "Well, perhaps you'd like to tell me how to adjust the graticules. I would like to know." Handing John a small screwdriver from his pocket, the airman explained the procedure, and John followed his instructions. Using the screwdriver on two slotted nuts on the gun sight, he realigned the aiming dot accurately over the sighting mark on the alignment board. Climbing out of the cockpit, he thanked both of his helpers and dismissed the airman. Walking back with the chief to his office, John said, "I believe that instrument fitter should have his eyesight checked by the MO before he does any more harmonisations, chief, don't you think?"

"Quite right, sir! We'll see to it, sharpish!" "What about the other aircraft?"

"Well, we shall just have to do them all in turn, at least the ones he been messing about with. I'll check all the records and let you know, sir." John went directly to the CO's office and reported the happenings to him.

"That certainly explains the poor scores you've been worried about. Glad that you have the situation in hand. Let me know how you get on this morning after your trip."

An hour later, John led a section of four aircraft up to the Fassburg air-to-ground gunnery range. Approaching there, he called up the range safety officer for permission to join the circuit. Receiving the okay, he set up the left-hand circuit pattern at three thousand feet altitude, checking the range as he did so. He noted the four ten-foot-square white targets, numbered one, two, three, and four from the left, and set up at an angle in front of the protective sandbanks, were all in order. He would be first to fire and would use target number one. Flying along the base leg at ninety degrees to the line of attack, he ran through the attack checklist, making sure the gun sight and cameras were switched on, and that he had a green light from the RSO, who was situated in the observation tower, well off to the right of the line of targets. Turning onto the attack path, he put the Venom into a thirty-degree dive toward the target, receiving a verbal permission from the RSO to open fire. Lining the target up in the gun sight, using the fixed cross and ring, not the gyro option, he quickly put the cross on the centre of the target, aiming a little high at first, and gently, with tiny, smooth adjustments, kept lowering it until it was centred. Everything felt just right. A quick squeeze on the trigger, mounted like a revolver trigger at the top of the pistol grip, and he felt the familiar slight shudder as the four 20 mm cannons fired off a short burst at six hundred rounds per minute per gun. He saw no flying sand or debris from around the target. This point coincided with the ideal height above the ground to fire and safely pull up, breaking off the attack. Pulling up into a climbing turn to the left away from the target, he completed the pattern and looked over to the left to see how the rest of his section was progressing. Something in his gut told him that that was a good pass, and he settled down to repeat the process until all his ammunition was exhausted; the others followed suit.

Once they had cleared the range and were returning to base, the range safety officer and his team went out to the targets and counted the holes in each one. To assist the scoring process, each aircraft had the tips of its ammunition rounds dipped in different coloured paint, red, blue, yellow, and green. As the round passed through the canvas, it left the telltale streak of colour on the target. The number of hits on each target was then telephoned immediately back to the squadron, and the individual scores were awaiting the eager pilots when they landed and returned to the crew room.

John found to his delight that he had just achieved the highest score he had ever made, and he quietly felt that the Venom was indeed a superb tool in this role. He, Norman, and the boss were all very interested in the other scores and found an unusual result appearing. Number four in the flight had made around about his average score; the other two had fared miserably, both being abysmally low, way below their normal average. John went immediately to the chief's office and pulled the records for the other three aircraft. Checking the dates, he found that two had very recently been harmonized; these were the ones with the low scores. They had also been harmonized by the poor-sighted instrument mechanic. He then suggested to the boss that a suitable remark, explaining the low scores, should be placed in the proper records of the affected pilots. He followed that by suggesting that he, personally, would assist the ground crew to reharmonize all the aircraft before they went on range again. Two days later the result was very marked; the whole squadron had improved very visibly, and John was called into the boss's office to be congratulated.

The boss had something else to impart and had been joined by the flight commanders and the adjutant. He began, "It seems one of the Fassberg Wing Venoms crashed earlier today, on the range." There was an immediate buzz of conversation, which subsided when Norman asked, "Did the RSO see what happened?" The boss replied, "Yes, and he said that it seemed that a wing came off during the recovery pull-up, after its attack on the target. That's all we know at the moment. Of course, the inquiry has already started, and when more is known we'll be informed. Meantime, the Venoms are grounded until the problem is resolved. We shall continue flying the Vampires we have left." That evening, in the bar, there was a great deal of speculation, and a great many drinks were consumed.

Two days later, a team arrived from the de Havilland factory at Hatfield. They were a team of mechanics headed up by one of the production line test pilots. With them, they carried the modification kits to install on the aircraft. The test pilot gave a briefing to all the pilots, explaining what the cause of the problem was and how the modification would cure it. Essentially, the new, thinner wing on the

Venom relied a great deal upon the stressed skin of the wing. With the great amount of low flying, high-g manoeuvres, cracks had developed around the cutout holes on the lower wing skin that allowed for the undercarriage legs to retract. The simple fix was to beef up the entire wing skinning around that area with carefully contoured slabs of high tensile alloy plate, strategically riveted into place. The works test pilot was there to prove each aircraft after it had been modified.

The program swung into action immediately, and a measure of confidence was regained by the squadron pilots. The whole episode was classified; after all, it concerned a major deficiency in NATO's first line of aerial defence, the Second Tactical Air Force. Within a week, John was joined by Paddy in the bar one evening. After a couple of drinks, they slipped out and went to John's room, where Paddy explained the situation. They had received a message that, in spite of all the security, the Russians had almost immediately come into possession of all the essential details. An asset we had in East Germany had indicated that he had a probable source of a highly sensitive nature that he needed to bring out personally, which could not be transmitted electronically for fear of interception.

"Of course, old lad," Paddy went on, "our masters have decided that he should be spirited out of there, by means they know not of! That, as you and I well know, means that 'Bat Airways' is called upon yet again."

"Crikey, it's been a while since our last sortie. What sort of condition is the Bat in?" John inquired.

"Even as we speak, the team has arrived and is going over it in fine detail. Of course, after your last episode with it, a lot of repair work was required; that was done immediately, and a couple of mods were carried out at the same time. The crew seems to think everything will be in great shape. Anyway, they want you to try it out tomorrow night, and if the kite's okay and we get the go-ahead, the 'op' is planned for the following night."

"Well, if it can throw some light on where the security leak is coming from, it's well worth the effort," John commented. "Just hope you can track the rotten sod down who's doing this to us."

"And so say all of us! " Paddy rejoined. "When we do catch the bastard, it will be a long time before he sees the light of day … if he ever does!" he added ominously.

TWENTY

The following evening, as dusk was falling, John cycled over to the Bat Hangar. There an enthusiastic ground crew greeted him with the customary ribald remarks. The early May evening was pleasantly warm with a light, broken cloud cover and a three-quarter moon, not quite bright enough to cast shadows, perfect for a night flight. As he did a preflight check, he congratulated the crew on the fine job they had done on repairing the previous damage. Then, without further ado, John climbed into the cockpit, did a quick cockpit check, and pressed the starter. A muffled "crack" ensued, and the engine instantly began to quietly idle in a perfectly tuned manner. John then switched on the sound-damping system, and the already very soft, gentle tickover and slight propeller noise faded away, leaving only the backwash of air to indicate any apparent indication of motion. *How the hell do they manage to do this*? John thought. *It makes a Rolls Royce sound like an old banger of a car by comparison*. He taxied to the takeoff point, checking all the controls and the engine instruments carefully as he went. Takeoff checklist completed, he turned on the smooth grass surface onto the runway heading and smoothly opened the throttle. The Tiger Moth responded instantly and with a very short run climbed gently away into the ever-fading twilight.

Some thirty minutes later he flew back over the landing area and was just able to make out the perimeter fence and the Bat Hangar in the soft moonlight; circling around, he made his approach and touched down softly, and, slowing quickly, taxied to the fence opening to the hangar. He parked the aircraft, ran the checklist, and shut down the engine. No one was in sight. He walked to the hangar office door, opened it, and walked into the well-lit interior, blinking in the bright light. "Blimey! Where did you spring from?" protested Bill. "You nearly gave me a heart attack! The prince of bloody darkness, that's what you are!"

"Well, somebody needs to keep you on your toes; if you're not charping it off, you're up to some skulduggery or the other!" John retorted. Looking around the assembled group, he saw they had been joined by Paddy, who greeted him with, "Hello me boy! How did your trip go, and how's the Bat flying tonight?"

"Went like a dream; it's as soft as silk out there. Lovely job you've done on the old girl, lads. Thanks very much indeed!" John answered, looking at the very earnest crew, who then seemed to relax.

"John, we need to talk," said Paddy. "Let's go into the inner office for a moment." Settling into the chair behind the desk, he waved to a nearby chair. "Pull up a pew, old lad." John sat down; Paddy looked at him and said, "How do you feel about doing an "op" tonight? I know it's very short notice, but there is a reason."

"First of all," John replied, "yes, I'm good to go. Not had a drink yet, and the weather looks good for the night. Visibility's okay! But tell me, why such short notice?"

"Security, in a word. There's an agent needs to come out with some 'hot' stuff. Now, through our usual channels we've set the pickup for the night after next. However, we have a good idea there's another 'mole' in the organization, and we want to avoid any mishaps. Your pickup was prebriefed as to this possibility when he opened his orders, just before a submarine in the Baltic dropped him off. Only he has been told of tonight's pickup location, so we believe you'll have a clean area for the job."

"If nothing goes amiss!" John interjected. "Sorry I interrupted, please go on." "Okay," Paddy continued, "assuming all goes well tonight, we have got some 'friends' to keep a watch on the area for the next two nights. They know nothing about tonight's op, but if they see any activity later, on the following nights, it will give us a good indication where our leak is situated. Now then, there's one other little 'goodie' I want to tell you about.

"You and I have realized that when you are on these missions, we have no means of communicating. Well, I believe we got the problem solved." As he said this, Paddy opened a rather large briefcase, pulled out two objects a little smaller than a house brick, and placed them on the table between them. "Guess what these are?"

"God only knows!" John expostulated, and then, looking harder, "it looks like an overgrown telephone without wires."

"Not a bad guess and not too far off the mark! They're something our boffin department has come up with, and there are only three of them in existence— these two and one that our agent has with him. Apart from the gent in 'Q' department at RAE who built them and we three, no one knows of their existence. Now! This is how they work. They have a built-in rechargeable battery, which can be switched off when they are not in use. Fully charged, as they are now, there's about twenty minutes of conversation time usable. Right? Remember that and don't chatter away, okay?"

"Got it!" came the terse reply.

"Now, when you are called, this green light comes on, and you get a low buzzing noise, which will be demonstrated in the next five minutes, at half past the hour. Ground to ground, the range is not great, up to half a mile or so, depending upon conditions, Air to ground, better with increasing altitude. In this region, being flat land hereabouts, you should get as much as five miles at five hundred feet. However, tonight we've gone one better. At this moment there's a Lincoln from Upwood stooging about, well on our side of the line doing nothing suspicious, at twenty thousand feet. He is acting as a relay for us, testing the system. From that height we should have an effective radius of about one hundred miles or so, ample for our needs."

"That's bloody marvellous!" John expostulated. "It means we can keep in touch, but, and it's a big *but*, how do we keep the opposition from listening in and, more importantly, tracking us?"

"Well, it uses a frequency that is way out of all normal communication channels and is *very* discreet. Now! These are the controls. So pay attention! This is the on/off switch: this is the green light I just mentioned, and this is the speech antenna," he said, pulling out a black knob on the top corner of the device, revealing a telescoping rod.

"Okay, if any one of us wishes to make a call, all you need to do is to switch on the phone and press this call button. This sends out a carrier wave signal to the other phones, and their green light comes on; the other two people pull out their antennaes, and that enables the speech facility. Remember also that it uses very little power to receive, but uses a lot to speak, so use conciseness, and don't chatter. Again, the less talk the more discreet the system is. For the same reason, try not to use military expressions and verbiage. Right?" John nodded in the affirmative.

"Now," Paddy continued, "the last little gizmo is this sliding panel on the back, and it is *very* important! Should you find yourself in an awkward predicament, it is a very useful 'destruct' facility. All you have to do is slide it open and push the little button beneath it. It will then explode in four seconds exactly and, I'm told, is a very powerful explosive indeed and will certainly kill anyone in a radius of ten feet and severely injure those within a twenty-foot circle. So! Don't bugger about with it—activate it, throw it, and then run like hell! Now! It's getting near test time, so stick it into your windbreaker, and let's step outside and give it a whirl. Oh yes, by the way, the lads here know nothing about this, so let's keep it between ourselves, okay!"

They stood outside in the mild evening air, some twenty yards from the hangar. Exactly on the half hour, John felt his radio phone vibrate. Looking down, he saw the green light glowing, and he switched on the "on" button, pulled out the antennae, and put the receiver's little holes to his ear. At the bottom, the little slots lined up with his mouth. Then he heard a very clear voice say, "Are we on for tonight?" John looked at Paddy, who said, "It's a winner."

"Good," came the reply, "is the magic carpet operator sober?" Paddy nodded at John to reply. "Good to go," John replied. "See you at the pub then," came the answer, and the green light on their phones went out.

Back inside the office, Paddy briefed John on the landing zone. "It's a quiet area, rather isolated. Just about a mile to the northeast of a little town called Calvorde. This is the layout. There's this big canal on the west side of town that runs northwest, then curves round to the west. Okay? As you can see, there's another, smaller canal running parallel to it, on the east side of the town. If you follow that one northeast for about a mile, you'll see it branches into a fork. That fork is the start of the landing zone, which lies on the north side of the left fork, which has a farm track running along the canal bank next to the field. There is a hedgerow of trees, and, off to the right, in the middle of the field is a large mature tree. Try not to run into it, eh? okay, to continue, as you approach, give our chappie on the ground a buzz on the phone; he will reply with a code word 'coffee' if it's a 'go' situation. If not, he will say, 'teapot.' That's a wave-off. Anything else is corrupt; just get out of there ASAP. Last of all, assuming it's 'coffee,' you can ask him for a 'Lucifer.' He will then give a quick flash with his torch, pointing towards the fork in the canals. That will give you an indication of where he is. After that, it's all up to you. Of course, as your bloody machine is so desperately quiet and invisible, he won't hear it; neither shall we on your return. We didn't hear you land just now, so, when you get back here, give me a call, and we shall be ready for you and have the gates open. Any questions?"

"Yes, do we know if there's been any farming activity on the field lately? These sodding farmers tend to leave their clobber all over the place, and I don't want a repeat of the last expedition!"

"No, we've got a clear field this time that was fallow for last year and grazed this year as well; rest your mind, there won't be any cattle on it tonight. All right?"

"Super. What's my ETA there?"

"It's set for 12:55 p.m. local time; I believe that will fit in nicely."

John did a quick calculation on the map, looked at the accompanying weather forecast, and said, "If I get airborne in fifteen minutes, it should all come together in the approved manner!"

Fifteen minutes later, he turned onto the westerly heading for takeoff. Climbing silently away, he turned onto his southeasterly course, levelling off at five hundred feet and paralleling the course of the Aller River until he crossed the Curtain line near Obisfelde. He could see the canal leading to Calvorde clearly in the moonlight and, a few minutes before his ETA, spotted the fork where the two canals joined. Looking around, he saw no activity on the roads or tracks and, feeling a little less tense, turned onto the approach, pressing the call button on his phone when he was lined up for landing. Almost immediately, he heard "coffee."

"Can you give me a Lucifer?" John asked, and at once he saw a flash of light halfway down his intended landing area. Easing back on power, he floated silently down to a smooth touchdown and rolled to a stop. Looking to his left, he saw a figure approaching steadily toward him. With his Browning Hi-Power in his right hand, he covered the man until he was alongside the aircraft. "Any chance of a lift, old lad?" the passenger enquired with a slight Lancashire accent. John relaxed a little and moved his finger off the trigger. The man climbed aboard without further ado and strapped in saying, "Christ, this thing is so damned quiet. I can't believe it!"

"Well, that's a fact," John replied. "Are you all set and comfortable?"

"Ready to go," came the reply.

A minute later, they rose silently into the air and set off on a dogleg course for Celle, not wanting to fly over the same flight path on the return trip. Again, the lights of Celle and smaller towns stood out in sharp contrast to the darkness of the eastern sector they were leaving behind. "Blimey," exclaimed the passenger. "It's lit up like Blackpool on Illumination Night!"

"Well, it certainly can be useful," John commented. "And it's not so abysmally dreary either." The remainder of the trip went uneventfully, and, about five minutes from landing, John pressed the call button on the phone and said, "Is the coffee shop open?"

The response came back immediately. "Anything for you, Squire! With or without sugar?" "With, if you please. I've got a sweet tooth tonight," John replied, indicating that "sugar," his passenger, was on board and well.

The landing run finished as he taxied through the open gate to the hangar. Coming to a halt, he switched off the engine as the ground crew manned each wingtip. Climbing out of the front cockpit, the passenger said to John, "Many thanks for the lift, my friend. Maybe I can return the favour one day!" As he stepped off the wing, he was ushered off to an awaiting Volkswagen by Paddy and disappeared into the night. Paddy came back to John, who handed him the phone. "This talking brick is a great piece of kit; whoever dreamt it up deserves a medal as big as a frying pan! Please thank him for me, would you?" "Be glad to, m'boyo," Paddy answered.

Three nights later, a Saturday evening, a roaring party was beginning in the Keller Bar. One of the pilots on 94 Squadron was celebrating his birthday, a splendid excuse for a bash. John entered the bar and spotted Paddy sitting at one end. He joined him, and Paddy asked, "What'll it be, then?"

"A large pint would go down very well at the moment. Thank you very much!"

"My pleasure. Your drinks are on me tonight." Drinks sampled, Paddy quietly said, "We got the word back today that the opposition have been running around like chickens with their heads off. Bloody marvelous, isn't it?" John nodded in agreement. "I'll look forward to hearing about our snitch, damn his eyes. Whoever it is, he needs to be dropped from a great height over the 'Oggin,' preferably midnorth Atlantic!"

The following Monday evening, about six thirty, a knock came on the door of John's room. "Come in," said John loudly as he was tying his shoelace. The door opened, and Paddy walked in. "Have a pew, mon ami! I'll be through in a minute; just gluing myself together for dinner." Paddy sat down in the green armchair. "Well!" he began. "We got the bugger this time. He fell for the bait—hook, line, and sinker!"

"Who was he? Anyone special?"

"As a matter of fact, he was. Another 'mandarin' of our esteemed civil service. A much-trusted dilettante of the Oxbridge persuasion, it would seem. Caught the sod red-handed, bad cess to him. He squealed like a pig during questioning, and the lads got some very good info on others of his ilk."

"That's marvelous. What do you think will happen to the rotten sod?"

"Well, he's certainly for the high jump! Once we've wrung him out thoroughly, it'll be up to the powers that be. I wouldn't be surprised to eventually read in the newspapers in a few months that he had committed suicide, whilst not of sound mind, in all probability!"

TWENTY-ONE

November 1954.

One morning, after the normal Met briefing for the wing of three squadrons was breaking up to go to their individual squadrons, and as the last few people were leaving the room, the wing commander flying drew John to one side, saying, "John, have you a moment for a quiet word?"

"Certainly, sir. Is there a problem?"

"Well, it all depends. Look, the question of your next posting has come up. You will recall that earlier this year we made a tacit agreement with the staff at Sylt that you would join them as one of their staff instructors at the end of your tour here on 145 Squadron?"

"Yes, sir."

"Well, HQ at Second TAF started the wheels in motion, when it all came to a grinding halt. Seemingly, postings at Air Ministry jumped on it and said no in a big way. Apparently, they have other plans for you. Anyway, the upshot is, they want you to toddle over to Adastral House and speak with them. They were very guarded about it and would not let our people know any of the details, and we've been told not to ask any question as to why!"

"Okay, sir. Thank you for telling me. When do they want me there?"

"As soon as possible, so this is what I'm arranging. A Vampire needs ferrying over to Benson. It will be ready to go tomorrow morning. You will be flying it. When you get to Benson, they will have a car waiting to run you up to the Airbox for your business there."

The next morning, John left Celle with a soft carryall containing some civilian clothing, which he stuffed into the small radio bay just behind the cockpit. The flight across Europe and the English Channel was uneventful, and he landed at RAF Benson. He was marshalled to a hangar, where he saw a black Humber Pullman limousine staff car waiting outside the hangar with an officer standing by its side. Climbing out of the Vampire, he handed the paperwork over to the ground crew after signing the form 700, then, collecting his carryall, he walked over towards the hangar office, where the officer who had been standing by the car joined him.

"Flying Officer Frazer?" the officer enquired.

"Yes, indeed. Can I help you?" came the reply.

"Yes. I have this car waiting for you. If you want to leave your flying clothing here you can change in the office; there is a toilet inside. Then we'll get you on your way. I'm told that you will be coming back through here when you return to your unit."

Twenty minutes later, John, having been ushered into the rear compartment of the Humber by its driver, was being driven through the nearby village of Wallingford in solitary state on his way to London. Upon arrival at Adastral House in Whitehall, just before lunchtime, he was directed to a small office in a remote part of the building. He knocked on the door and heard, "Come in!" Opening the door, he saw a familiar figure rising from the chair behind the desk. It was his old friend Geoff Sanders, dressed in civilian clothes. Shaking John's hand, he motioned to an easy chair.

"John, good to see you. Come on in and take a pew; it's good to see you again. I've been hearing all about your escapades from Paddy, who keeps me well informed."

Sitting down, John said, "Thank you, Geoff; it's good to see you again. I daresay that you are the one I should thank for the VIP treatment coming here?"

"Correct! In addition, it's a pleasure! Now, you are probably wondering what this is all about?"

"I'm curious, to say the least, but I've learned not to ask questions."

"Good for you! That avoids unnecessary complications, doesn't it? Let's get straight down to it and not waste time. As you now know, the question of your next posting has arisen, and, of course, need I say, we have plans for you."

"I'm listening, sir, just hoping it's not too awful."

"Well, I don't think you'll find it too onerous. Now, as you know, Fighter Command is reequipping with a new fighter, the Hawker Hunter. They're already in operation at OCU at RAF Chivenor, as you probably know, and at some of the squadrons. Now then, next year, the OCU at Pembrey is also going to have a Hunter flight in addition to the Vampires there. You will be one of the Hunter instructors. This is not something we arranged; you really were singled out for the instructor's slot. They need someone with your ground attack experience and expertise."

"Nice to know one is wanted!" John exclaimed. "But what else is in store for me?" A knock came on the door, and, after Geoff had said, "Come in," a waiter entered pushing a small cart with some covered dishes and a pot of coffee on it.

"Thought a spot of lunch here might not go amiss; you're probably quite peckish."

"I certainly could eat a bite or two. Thank you, that's very kind."

"Not at all. As a matter of fact, it's also a means of me briefing you about other things, in private, where we won't be overheard."

After they had finished eating, Geoff said, "We'd best be on our way now. We're going to drive down to the Manor, and I need to be there by three o'clock." They walked through the corridors down to the courtyard, where the Humber was waiting with the driver holding open the rear door. They climbed in and settled down, in great comfort, separated from the driver by a substantial partition with a thick glass screen, and the car drew smoothly away through the imposing gateway into the London traffic. As they proceeded, John remarked, "Well, Geoff, it seems you've moved on up in the scheme of things. This is pretty splendid transportation. Should I be calling you 'Sir Geoffrey'?"

"Not necessary; let's just keep it at Geoff."

"Thank you. That makes me feel comfortable."

"Well, you've become one of 'the family,' so to speak, and it's a pretty small group, I can assure you."

As they drove through the suburbs of Greater London and into the countryside, Geoff continued to outline to John what lay ahead for him: "Your posting to Pembrey was fortuitous for us, as I said before. It pleases the Flying Branch and, for once, doesn't clash with our plans for you. Now, here's what the outline is. We have an emerging political problem arising. The IRA, which for many years now has been somewhat benign, has undergone a radical change within the last couple of years. It has literally been taken over by a very determined body of hardcore Communists who will exacerbate the romantic ideals of the movement to work against this country in every way. These people are not idealists for the Irish people, as such. They do not hesitate to kill or maim their own members in order to establish complete authority. They are simply after raw power and total control over the greater mass of our communities here in the West. They intend to do so by creating acts of terror within the communities they purport to glorify and use them as martyrs to the cause. They are going forward with people who have been, and are currently being, trained in Moscow and will be supplied with arms by that source. Sadly, we believe that a lot of the funding for this movement is being raised in America by various groups there who are sympathetic to the various long-standing Irish 'causes' and who are oblivious to the real motives behind the movement and do not begin to comprehend the trauma they will, unwittingly, help to create.

That's the overall picture. Now, why do we need you in Pembrey? Understand; their movement is short of weaponry—small arms of any variety and larger explosives. At this time, they are attempting to ship such materials into Ireland and have run afoul of the Irish customs services, who are working with us, begrudgingly perhaps, but they are just as well aware of the problem and worried by it. You see, the IRA has now declared that it does not just wish to remove the British government from Northern Ireland, but all existing forms of government in all of Ireland, and replace it with a Socialist one-party state, and we all know what that means! As I said, they are after arms, by any means. Pembrey is rather unique, geographically speaking. Believe it or not, it has seven miles of very flat, firm, sandy shore. Very tidal, yes. However, it has a wide expanse of flat, firm sand, perfect for landing, day or night, from the sea by infiltrating parties. The station armoury alone, with some four hundred Lee Enfield .303 rifles and pistols, complete with God knows how much ammo, besides a fair number of Bren guns and Sten guns, plus air-to-ground rockets, makes it a prime target. Now, just next door to Pembrey, across the estuary of the River Towy, lies Pendine Sands, well known to the public at large and famous worldwide as a venue for attempts upon a variety of record-breaking speed trials. It is better known to the military as one of our major ordnance testing ranges. The army facility there already has its security systems at a high degree of alertness. At Pembrey, we have a rather more subtle problem. The beach, although on government property, has certain bylaws for the surrounding fishermen. This group is very benign, but they do use the beach for fishing extensively! We do not wish to alarm them or upset them by barring their long-standing access. The further facet of the problem is the very left wing and vocal trade unions of the mining and docking industries of the local coal mining area of South Wales and its attendant major shipping ports. The majority of their trade union officials are card-carrying members of the British Communist Party. That is a fact! They make no secret about it. Therefore, as you can see, at Pembrey we are sitting on a powder keg!"

At the Manor, during the afternoon, John's briefings continued. Later, over dinner, Geoff told John of the immediate plans for him on his return to Celle. "We are sending you on yet another course! This one is rather special. It is a winter survival course but differs considerably from the usual run of things. A small, select group of personnel, RAF and army, will be going down into the Bavarian Alps to a little town, just over the German border, in Austria. You won't be told the name of the place until you get there. You and a couple of others from your base will travel down by train to Munich. There you will join the others in your group, and you will all meet your group leader, who is quite a forceful person and greatly experienced in the dark arts of escape and evasion! He will accompany you to your destination, get you settled in for the first couple of days, and then depart, leaving you to the mercy of your instructors. You will be there for two weeks only, and it will be quite intensive. You will travel there and remain in civilian clothes for the whole period. The rest of it you will find out about at the time. Any questions?"

A day or so after his return to Celle, John was called into the boss's office. "Well, it seems you're off again on yet another course, Johnny. A couple of others from here are going with you, and you'll be leaving on Saturday. Here are the written instructions and your railway warrant. It seems you are much in demand these days! By the way, did you get any inkling of what your next posting will be when you were over at Air Ministry?"

"Not specifically, sir; they were a bit tight-lipped about it, but it does sound as if I'm going onto the Hunter."

"Lucky young so and so! Did they indicate a squadron or an OCU?"

"Not specifically, again, sir. I did get the feeling that it might be an OCU slot, however."

"Well, count yourself lucky to get a flying job; they're in short demand at present, so I'm told by a friend of mine at HQ."

On the following Saturday, early in the afternoon, the small group of travellers from Celle disembarked from the train at Munich. From an adjoining compartment on their train, an older man, who carried a distinct air of authority about him, joined them. He greeted them. "Good afternoon, gentlemen. My name is Neave, and I'm the chap in charge of you. I'm giving you your tickets for our destination, which is Ehrwald, in Austria, just over the border from Garmisch-Partenkirchen. I know none of you have your passports with you; all you have are your Form 1250 RAF identity cards. That's okay. I'll be handling the border control people when we get there. We're going to go over to another platform to catch the onward train, and we should meet up with the rest of our group at that time. We have our own coach reserved on the next train, and I will know which coach is ours. Now! Follow me, and don't chatter too much or you'll sound like a bunch of old women! Don't all walk around together in a group, either. Break up and go individually but keep me in sight."

They dutifully followed him and on arrival at the platform saw a similar group to themselves. Neave approached that group and spoke with them, presumably giving them the same preamble they had just received. Some ten minutes later, their train drew into the station, exactly on time. Neave was standing in exactly the correct spot for boarding the correct carriage, which was a rather splendid old Rheingold Express first-class saloon car, a leftover from the prewar Bavarian Railway, which had somehow survived the hostilities. They boarded, carrying their luggage with them, and settled down in the quite luxurious surroundings. John thought to himself, *Whoever this chap is, he certainly does things in style!*

Once under way, Neave stood and addressed the assembled crew. He pointed out that Austria had only recently freed itself from the clutches of the Russian Occupying Forces and their Communist control. Hence, they were somewhat leery about foreign troops on their soil, and hence the "civvie" attire they were wearing. He went on to say that they would be staying in a somewhat remote Gasthaus situated some two kilometres from Ehrwald and, again, would have the entire place to themselves for the duration of their stay. The train wound on through the increasingly mountainous and scenic countryside. It ground to a halt at Garmisch-Partenkirchen and, after a brief stop, continued on its journey south toward its destination at Innsbruck. Neave was on his feet adding a few more details, when the door at the end of the carriage opened and, without ceremony, in walked the train conductor accompanied by an Austrian Border Control officer. Neave erupted in an enraged outburst of fluent German, soundly berating them for disturbing his lecture on protocol and correct behaviour whilst in Austria. Their conduct, he stated in no uncertain terms, was reprehensible and a disgrace! This group and the carriage had the highest diplomatic clearances, and this was a serious intrusion and an insult. He added that their superiors would be hearing about this great affront to diplomacy. The two officials spluttered profuse apologies and, with much heel clicking, withdrew.

"That, gentlemen," Neave continued in a very calm and quiet manner, "is the way to bluff your way through a lot of situations, particularly with very regimented people who are used to being bossed around. You will have noticed, of course, that they were so surprised and embarrassed that they totally forgot to ask us for our tickets or, perhaps more importantly, any form of identification! That, perhaps, can serve as lesson number one on this course! Evasion can take many forms, including pretending to be someone very important."

The short journey to Ehrwald soon passed, and as dusk was falling, the train came to a halt, and they disembarked. Outside the station a small bus awaited; they climbed aboard, and it sedately set off to wind its way out of the small Tyrolean town onto a narrow, twisting road climbing up into a mountain pass. Precisely two kilometres later, it jerked to a halt outside the Gasthaus that was to be their home for the next two weeks. They scrambled off and lugged their kit up a flight of steps and into the accommodation. Dumping their kit in the old wooden-planked entrance hall, they were led into a warm and homely dining room by the host, who was a large and genial-looking man about fifty years of age. Once seated they were served dinner by two robust and rather matronly women. The food was plain and of good quality and very generous in quantity. As an added bonus, they were served with large steins of good Bavarian beer.

Dinner plates were then cleared away and steins were refilled, and Neave got to his feet to address them yet again. He began by explaining that during the first week they would all be taught to ski to a reasonable degree of proficiency. The coach they arrived on they would not see again until they departed to return to their units. Their means of transport for the next two weeks would be skis or on foot. The day would begin after an early breakfast, after which they would travel cross-country, on skis, to the nursery slopes in the town. They would be given skiing instruction all morning. At eleven o'clock, they would return, cross-country again, to the inn for lunch. At one o'clock, a return to the slopes would be made for another session of skiing lessons. At four o'clock, they would return to the inn for supper at five, followed by a short break, then, starting at seven, two hours of lectures on escape, evasion, and survival techniques! Presumably they would feel in the need of sleep by then, but, if they felt so inclined, they were quite free to walk down the road into town for a look at the nightlife!

He then introduced them to their host, Hans, a very sturdy and genial person who had a remarkable tale to tell. Although an Austrian, whose family had always lived here in Ehrwald, one year after the outbreak of the war, following the German takeover and occupation of Austria, he was conscripted into the German Wehrmacht. At the outbreak of the offensive against Russia, he was sent to the Russian front in the German attack into the Caucuses. He was captured by the Russians and, in company with many other prisoners, began the long march eastward into captivity. After two months, during the Russian retreat, they were about twelve hundred kilometres from Austria when they came under an air attack by an element of German fighters. Their escorts fled for cover, so did the prisoners, and in the confusion he managed to conceal himself well away from the others in the group. The guards then commenced to round up the prisoners, shooting not only the German wounded, but also those of their own who could not walk. Because they wanted to keep moving to avoid capture by the oncoming German forces, they moved off, leaving him amongst the dead. He lay motionless as another body of prisoners and their captors passed. Night was falling rapidly as he planned his next moves. A little to the south he had noticed a ruined farmhouse with a barn, which was still intact. Under cover of darkness he carefully made his way to it and found it empty except for a half empty sack of potatoes and a loft above containing a fair quantity of straw. Half starved, he eagerly devoured a quantity of potatoes, climbed into the loft, and fell asleep. He awoke next day and realized the place was swarming with Russian troops, who proceeded to search the place—in the process, jabbing at the straw covering him with a pitchfork. By some miracle they missed him and left a couple of hours later, having taken a break for their midday meal.

After they left, he made his plans. He would travel only at night and avoid all contact with anyone, avoiding villages and towns. He would remove all evidence of anything military from his clothing and would replace it all with ordinary Russian peasant items whenever he could acquire them. He also decided that he would avoid any German military outfits as well. His reasoning was that, disguised as a peasant and unable to speak any Russian, they would probably treat him as a deserter and shoot him out of hand. If that did not occur, then he would simply be put back into uniform and forced into combat again with the very strong possibility of being killed or captured by the Russians yet again.

During the next eight months, he carefully made his way westward, crossing Romania then Hungary. Toward the end of this time, he noticed that the movement of Germans eastward had ceased; in fact, some units appeared to be pulling back to the west. One day as the sun came up behind him and he was settling in to rest until nightfall, he saw the morning light glistening on some far-off snowcapped mountain peaks. He had already crossed the Carpathian range of mountains in Romania, so what he was looking at was his beloved Alps in Austria. A pang of joy went through him and gave him new hope and strength. A month later, high up in the mountains, above the tree line, he looked down upon his hometown of Ehrwald. For the next few days, he carefully watched the activity below. He saw quite a lot of military activity in progress; then one morning he heard far-off gunfire. This was not small-arms fire but heavy artillery. He continued his vigil.

Two days later, he noticed frantic movements below. Over the last day and night, the gunfire had become louder, presumably because of this, and the Germans below were obviously planning to withdraw. They did, and later that afternoon he saw some unfamiliar vehicles and helmeted troops pull into the town. They were not Russians; this he could tell easily—firstly their clothing was very different, and secondly they came from the west. The following morning, looking down on the town centre, he saw a small ceremony taking place. A flag was being run up the flagpole; it was the Stars and Stripes of the Americans. A wave of joy surged through his being, followed by a pang of anxiety. Would they consider him a prisoner of war or possibly a war criminal? For two more days, he agonized over this dilemma. The following morning, he decided to move, come what may. He made his way down to a house on the outskirts, which belonged to a cousin. Arriving there, he calmly walked in through the back door. His cousin's wife turned, looked at him, dropped the pan she was holding, letting out a stream of joyous chatter, and threw her arms around his neck, hugging him to her. Later, when things had calmed down, he learned what had taken place since he left and what was happening now.

His cousin had also been drafted into the German forces and had been killed in action. He himself was reported missing and presumably dead. The landings in France had taken place, and the Allied forces had fought their way into Germany; the Russians had carried out huge offences in the East, and Germany was on its knees. The American troops were extremely friendly, giving away all sorts of things to the locals, including a great deal of sweets, chocolate bars, and chewing gum to the delighted children. She had heard from the local police chief, who was another cousin, that the main fighting troops had moved on, and those left behind, who were now in charge, were mainly interested in tracking down anyone who had affiliations to the Nazi Party. Armed with this knowledge, he bathed and shaved for the first time in months, then, having changed into some of his cousin's clothes, made his way into the town centre to the police station. He entered, and the elderly constable on duty stared in amazement at him. "Hans," he cried, "you've returned from the dead!" The hubbub brought the chief out of his office, and a joyous reunion ensued. The upshot of it all, some weeks later, all the questions of his thrilling and gruelling experience being told, his exploits were duly discovered by the Americans in charge. They were trying to reestablish local Austrian control and government. He had become a local legend by this time, and as the reconstruction took place, he was duly elected mayor by the townspeople and remained as such until the present.

John's group listened in awe to this tale, and they were then introduced to their skiing instructors, who were all locals and Austrian army reservists. John's group was to discover they had almost been born on skis and seemed more at home on them than they were walking about. To a man, they idolized Hans and had learned many of their own survival skills from him. The next couple of days proved very gruelling to everyone in the group. Many little-used muscles and tendons ached abominably, and after the evening of lectures, accompanied by a great intake of food and beer, the students fell gratefully into bed to sleep very soundly until the next session of strenuous activity the following day. Toward the end of the week, their fitness having improved remarkably, John and some others ventured down into the town in the evening to look around. Up until then, they had confined themselves to the ski slopes and to the ski lodge, restaurant, and bar situated at the foot of the ski lift to the upper slopes. They had also discovered the restorative qualities of hot Gluvine, which they enjoyed perhaps a little to excess. During the short evening in the town, John took note of the layout and important buildings. Some idea of what might be happening the following week had begun to form in his mind. He said nothing but observed a lot.

Saturday saw their final morning of skiing, and at lunchtime all were awarded bronze proficiency medallions. Following this was a big celebratory dinner at their lodge, which turned into quite a party. On Sunday, they were briefed on the next phase.

Essentially, the next day, Monday, they would be conducted to the top of the local ski lift dressed in their flying gear, which included a Scandinavian string vest and special cold-weather undergarments. They also carried their escape kits, which were standard survival gear packed in their ordinary parachute packs. The parachute materiel itself could be utilised to provide a makeshift tent. They were then to make their way cross-country, above the tree line, to another ski lift summit. They were to be there two days hence at noon, to be met by an instructor, who would check them in and send them on their way back to the point of origin, near to the foot of the ski slopes in the town itself. They would then check in at the entrance of the Gasthaus on the church square. Of course, during the whole time the local authorities would be on the lookout for them. If spotted, they would be duly captured and then interrogated.

TWENTY-TWO

John had decided on his plan well before they were sent off at the top of the ski lift. They were dispatched individually, at intervals. When his turn came, he disappeared from the site and immediately took cover behind an outcrop of ice-covered rock, where he settled down out of sight. Two hours passed, and he then stripped off his flying suit, revealing his civilian skiing gear beneath. From his emergency pack he removed a lightweight holdall backpack, into which he folded his flying suit and from it took out his camera, a 35 mm Leica he had acquired a year ago from a friend who urgently needed some cash to pay his mess bill. Slinging the camera around his neck, he then made his way back toward the ski lift drop-off point. His arrival there coincided with the next of the day's skiers arriving at the summit. As they dropped off the T bar, he swung onto it, exclaiming, "Danke Schon." He rode back to the base of the lift and walked gently into the town. He called in at a photographic shop in the church square, where he purchased an impressive wide-angle lens attachment for his camera, a couple of rolls of film, and a leather camera case and strap to hold it all. From there he strolled to the railway station, where he examined the timetable for trains going north into Germany. Next, he walked to a small, cosy, and rather inconspicuous Gasthof situated in a side street. He checked in, posing as a freelance photographer from England who was taking scenic pictures for a British skiing magazine. He had taken the precaution of phoning them the previous evening to make a reservation, ascertaining at the same time that they would accept payment for his stay with his cheque written on his account at Lloyds, Cox & Kings branch, in London. Having settled in his room, he slipped out into the town again, unobtrusively blending in with the other tourists. As he meandered, he practiced his "street skills" taught at the Manor, constantly scanning for anyone who might recognize him. On his way, he located certain buildings, and from vantage points in a couple of cafes, observed the comings and goings of their occupants. He then retired for the rest of the day, taking dinner in the guesthouse. He spent the Tuesday doing much the same, pretending to take snapshots as he did so, and further increasing his knowledge of the day-to-day operation and conduct of the town.

On Wednesday morning, he was up quite early and had a large breakfast before stepping out to catch a bus, which would take him to the ski lift where they were to rendezvous at noon. He arrived there to find it just starting operations for the day and caught the first T-bar to the summit. Stepping off at the top, he scanned the area and saw that it was situated just at the top of the tree line. He looked to the west and walked off in that direction, staying in the trees. He found a spot, well concealed, where he could observe the ski lift and the approach from the west. He then took off his backpack and took out his flying suit, which he donned. Then, having also removed his survival gear, he packed away his camera equipment. Next, he rolled around in the snow, working his way down to the soil. Kneeling in the dirt, he rubbed a little on his face. He had purposely not bathed or shaved since departing the lodge on Monday morning, and he rapidly acquired a somewhat dishevelled appearance. Then he sat and waited. At eleven thirty, two of the instructors stepped off the lift, looked around, and then went over to a bench, where they could look out westward for incoming people. John had earlier assumed that they would do this and had picked out a handy, well-concealed spot in the trees where he would be slightly behind them. Quietly, taking his kit with him, he made his way through the trees to that spot and sat down on a log to await developments. At about twelve thirty, a figure came into view coming from the west, making its way slowly toward them. John then slipped quietly out of cover and came quietly up behind the two instructors, who were talking and paying rapt attention to the approaching figure, still half a mile away.

"Guten Tag! Mien Herr, wie geht es dir?" John said quietly, standing about two feet behind them. Both gave a start and swung round. Seeing John, they burst into laughter.

"Oh, it is you," said one. "But where have you come from? We did not see you."

"Ah! Well, that would be telling, wouldn't it?" John retorted. "Now you can check me off on your list. Correct?"

"Of course! You are the first to arrive. This is very gut!" came the reply. Then, pointing to the west, John said, "Look! I can see someone coming. And isn't that another figure farther off on the horizon, higher up the slope?" The two instructors were searching for the other figure, which was nonexistent. John had simply made the statement to distract them. Whilst they were concentrating so hard on both the approaching figure and the nonexistent one, John sidled quietly away from them to the rear and back to his cover, where he slipped out of his flying suit and transformed himself back to the photographer's guise. By this time, the lonely figure from the west was approaching the instructors and fully occupied their attention. Slipping from his cover, John walked calmly over to the ski lift and gently boarded a T-bar that a skier was just vacating, rode to the bottom of the lift, and caught the next bus back into town.

Saturday morning saw John depart very early from his accommodation of the last five days, without taking breakfast, and saunter over to the Gasthaus on the church square, the final "check-in" point. Just off the main hall and reception were the toilets. He went into the men's room, entered a booth, and again reverted to his flying suit and escape garb. This done, he sauntered out into the main hall and took a seat to await events. He did not have to wait long. Some ten minutes later, Neave and the two instructors John had spoken to on Wednesday came into the hotel hallway to see John sitting, waiting for them. "Mien Gott!" exclaimed Otto, one of the instructors. "It's him again, the Phantom!" Neave burst out laughing and exclaimed, "Johnny, it seems you've done it again—first past the post and ahead of schedule to boot!"

"How have the others got on?" John enquired.

"Well, some of them made it to the first checkpoint, but most have been captured. We've just two others to check in, and that'll be it. Now, while we wait for them, I'd like to debrief you. Let's go over there out of the way. I expect you would like a cup of coffee."

They sat on a settee, and coffee was served to them while Neave enquired about the exercise. John told him that he had experienced few problems and that he was sure the previous training he had received had been of great value. He then mentioned that if this had been a "for-real" situation, he would have made for the old Luftwaffe airfield at Landsberg, to the west of Munich, where he would have stolen an aircraft to make his escape.

Neave nodded in approval, and then John added, almost as an afterthought, "To cover my getaway from here, I would have caused some confusion."

"And how would you have done that, pray?" asked Neave.

"Well, first of all, I would have taken some explosive charges they have stored in the local military reserve outfit here in town after I had disabled their vehicles. Then I would have placed charges, with timers, in the telephone exchange, and the police station, disabling their cars as well, then the transformer grid in the power company yard, and, last of all, one under the main signal box at the railway station—the last one timed to go off an hour after the departure of the train I would have left town on."

Neave looked at John sceptically and asked, "Really, and how would you have done all that without being caught in the act?"

"Well, actually, if you go and look in all those places, you will see I've already done it. I certainly have not placed any real charges, but I have left notes everywhere with all the appropriate timings."

"Really! I'll be damned, and you didn't get caught?"

"No, sir, I did not!"

"Well, I'd love to hear the details."

John grinned wryly, saying, "Well now, that's my little secret!" Their conversation broke off there as a police car drew up outside, and from it emerged a policeman and the two other survivors, who, they shortly discovered, had been captured on the outskirts of the town. The exercise now over, Neave, John, and the other two went out to the small bus awaiting them and returned to their lodgings for a much-needed shower, shave, change of clothing, and a very hearty breakfast.

Back at Celle, a week or so later, John saw Paddy in the bar one evening. They sat quietly at a table. "Well, me boyo! You seem to have created quite an impression in certain quarters," Paddy began.

"Oh! Really? Do tell. Nothing too detrimental, I hope."

"Far from it! It would seem that a certain Mr. Neave was most impressed with your performance, so George informed me. He seemed particularly interested in your ability to suddenly appear somewhere for a rendezvous or whatever and then mystically disappear! How do you do that, anyway?"

"Ah, well! That's my tradecraft secret, and the Magicians Union would not be pleased with me if I told you!" John retorted.

"Likewise, he thought your leaving notes everywhere to explain what you had done was very impressive. They did check it all out and found that by the time the last charge would have gone off, at the railway station, you would have been safely over the border in Germany!"

"So, it did work out quite well then?" John said. "No other repercussions, I hope?"

"Not at all! Although, he did think it was a bit cheeky signing each note with 'The Phantom Farter strikes again!' The mayor there was highly amused, but it seems he has smartened up his security since!"

"I do have a question, Paddy," John enquired. "Just who is this bloke Neave? I seem to know the name but can't place him."

"Okay, perhaps the penny will drop when I say that he is the original 'Great Escaper'; you'll probably recall that he was an army officer captured at Dieppe as France was collapsing. Later, he was the first POW to escape from Colditz Castle. He was then recaptured but managed to escape yet again, making his way back to the UK. He was the first chap to do so! He then went on to help train aircrew in ways to escape in occupied territory. He went into intelligence and, finally, was elected as an MP for Abingdon. This exercise you were on was the first in what we hope would be an ongoing programme. We had tried to continue after the war, but the previous government put the kybosh on that.

"Presumably Moscow didn't approve!" Paddy added with a note of disdain.

Two days later, Paddy was back in London sitting in George's office. George opened the discussion. "Sorry to bring you back here at short notice, Paddy, but something has cropped up that we need to talk about. Our Bat programme."

"So, what's up? Have we been found out?" Paddy queried.

"No; however, questions are being asked in certain quarters as to the means by which we 'spirit' agents in and out without 'their' knowledge. 'They' do not like this, and presumably 'their' friends in the opposition don't like it either."

"I can see how that would disturb them, but the opposition must know we use an aircraft. After all they have had contact, and shots have been exchanged in anger!" Paddy chimed in.

"Indeed, but they are mystified by the details surrounding the whole operation. As you know, we've caught three major 'leaks,' and this troubles certain people, and they are becoming restive! None of which is good for us. To give you some idea, this very office was found 'bugged' yesterday morning on a routine sweep. I have taken the precaution to have it swept again this morning, only an hour ago. They didn't find anything, but we are now in a high state of alert."

"So, what are we planning to do about it?"

"Well, Paddy, as I see it, we have no alternative other than closing down the programme immediately."

"Christ! That's a blow, but I can see the problem. If the powers-that-be start probing around, there's a lot of secret know-how at stake."

"Exactly! The advanced technology involved in the Bat is all very new development, and the "opposition" would give up the Czar's crown jewels for it. It's simply too risky to continue. Apart from enemy action, even a crash or pileup on friendly territory would be catastrophic, to say the least. Too many probing questions, by far. Anyway, our masters have shut us down as of yesterday, and we're to make it all disappear. It is now a myth, a mere figment of someone's imagination."

"So, I expect you will want me to tell our intrepid aviator, right?" Paddy enquired as Geoff nodded an affirmative. Then he went on, "What about the engineers over there?"

"I alerted them yesterday, and they started to dismantle it at once. By the time you get back, it will be history. The very small, sensitive bits will be returned to Farnborough, whence they came. All the rest is to be cut up and scrapped. The Tiger Moth will be returned to its original state and disappear from Celle. We need John to do one last 'moonlight flit' and fly it down to Buckeberg, where it will go back into the system to be scrapped. Any problems with that, Paddy?"

"Not a bit of it, Geoff. I'll drive down there myself to make the arrangements and pick up his nibs. What do I tell him, by the way, and what do we have in store for him?"

"You can tell him everything I've told you; we know we can trust him completely. Now, I've been talking to those on high about his future. He's a valuable asset, and his flying skills mean that he is in demand, so his posting to Pembrey is as we wanted. He is due to go there early next year, beginning of March in fact, at the normal time for his end of tour at Celle. That way it will seem routine and no questions asked. Before then, however, we need him over here at the Manor for some more training and a very thorough briefing on his next assignment. He has a lot of leave accumulated, so I suggest he applies for leave over Christmas and New Year, prior to starting his courses in January. Then we'll send him back to his unit for February, and he'll finally depart from there at the end of the month."

Friday, December 3. Paddy had returned to Celle and had briefed John on all the details of his discussion with Geoff. However, since his return from London the situation had changed somewhat; John's posting notice had come through the system. His posting to Pembrey was to take effect from the fifteenth of February. Prior to that date, he was to take three weeks of leave, which would include terminal leave and accumulated annual leave, commencing Monday the twentieth of December. On Monday the third of January 1955, he was to report to Air Ministry to begin a series of courses, the nature of which was not disclosed. Paddy went on to say, "If you feel like it, I'd like to get the Tiger Moth down to Buckeberg tonight. Would a departure at about six o'clock this evening be okay?"

"Don't see why not; it's dark at five, and the airfield here will be shut down for the weekend. Weather shouldn't be a problem," John concurred.

"Right, then; we're on! The lads will be at the hangar to see you off. I'll start there now and will arrange for your arrival. When you arrive we'll have a quick bite in the mess there, and then I'll drive us back here. All being well, we should get here about nine-ish in time for a noggin or two!"

On arrival at the hangar, he could see in the dappled moonlight the Tiger Moth standing outside. Next to it stood a one-ton Austin K9 truck with a canvas-covered body. Ginger and a couple of others, all wearing RAF uniforms, greeted him. He handed them his bicycle and asked them to be good enough to drop it off outside the mess for him. They then told him the hangar was totally cleared out; no evidence of them remained there. He turned to the aircraft and saw it was now just a standard Tiger Moth, complete with normal tires and a two-bladed wooden propeller; however, the tailwheel cum skid remained. Looking in the cockpit, everything was back to normal, and in the rear bucket seat sat a standard parachute and dinghy pack. He climbed aboard, strapped in, then said to Ginger, who was standing at the cockpit side, "Thank the lads for all you have done for me on these capers, I really do appreciate it so very much."

"Bless your heart, sir; it's been a real pleasure. Good luck!" Ginger replied and walked around the port wing to the nose of the aircraft, ready to hand swing the propeller to start the engine.

The short flight to Buckeberg was uneventful; however, John was amazed at how noisy the Bat had become, and the performance seemed quite sluggish with the primitive propeller. The one wonderful legacy left was the smooth running, beautifully balanced engine. Good to his word, Paddy was there to meet him on landing. After John had handed over the aircraft to the ground crew, Paddy led him directly to his car nearby. John peeled off his leather, lamb's wool lined Irvin flying jacket and flying suit, revealing his civvie clothes beneath. They climbed into the car, and Paddy set off for Celle. During the journey, an idea had been forming in John's mind.

"Paddy," he asked, "with regard to the dear old Bat, I've heard that they are selling them off to various flying clubs and other organizations in the UK. Do you know anything about that?"

"I really don't know. Why? What have you got in mind?"

"Well, it occurs to me that if it's going back to some MU in the UK for disposal, someone will have to fly it back. If that's the case, I'd like to be the one to do so, if we can arrange it without drawing undue notice to ourselves."

"I'll quietly check into it and see what we can do. Putting two and two together, I suppose you'd like to fly it back when you leave Celle. Right?"

Smiling to himself, John nodded. "Precisely! And thanks, it would be a nice way to go."

TWENTY-THREE

It had been a hectic week of partying for John's farewell from the squadron, and, feeling rather worse for wear, he was driven to the railway station on the morning of Sunday the nineteenth of December to board the Blue Train for the Hook of Holland en route to the United Kingdom. Once installed in a compartment, he relaxed as the train pulled away to the south on its way toward Hanover and then on to a scheduled stop at Buckeberg. Almost at once after leaving the station the train passed by the airfield, lying to the west. John saw the branch line leading off to the south side of the airfield, the path that had led him back to safety so often. The memories flooded in. What an incredible two years he had spent here; so much had happened. There were so many happy times and a few sad ones, others he could not talk about except with those involved, but what lay ahead?

As the train rolled along, he began to think about the immediate plan. He was to leave the train at Buckeberg, where he would be met by Paddy and driven to the mess where he would spend the night. As he mused on all that lay ahead, the refreshment cart came down the corridor. As it paused outside his compartment, he purchased a much-needed cup of excellent coffee, returned to his window seat, and opened a novel he was reading. It was *Live and Let Die*, about a spy called James Bond, written by Ian Fleming, an author who was all the rage. His first novel, *Casino Royale*, had been published the previous year, 1953, and was an instant success. *Live and Let Die* was a splendid follow-on. The

Bond character was all that any swashbuckling hero of fiction should be. John thought wryly how glamorous Fleming made it all appear. So different to the rather mundane and sometimes sordidly plain and dirty his own unglamorous little episodes had been. As he mused on these things, he drifted off to sleep, leaving the coffee, still half full, to go cold.

It seemed to him only an instant later when he felt the train's brakes go on, and it started to slow. The guard came down the corridor, opened the compartment door, and announced that they were arriving at Buckeberg. John took his two suitcases down from the luggage rack and made his way to the carriage door as the train came to a halt at the platform. He dismounted and looked toward the exit, where he saw Paddy waiting for him. As they drove to the officers mess, Paddy quizzed John. "You're looking a bit seedy. What's up?"

"I think I'm partied out; the last few nights have been hectic, to say the least."

"Well, don't worry, old son, a good night's sleep will fix you up fine. I've booked you a room in the mess tonight. Then you can set forth tomorrow on your trip." Over dinner, Paddy told him that he had also arranged for him to stop at Butzweilerhof the following day to refuel and spend the night there, as he had requested. The next day he would fly on to Calais, where refuelling arrangements had been made at the airport. From there he would continue across the channel to England and then on to his final destination at Wymeswold. "The people at the MU there will take the Bat off your hands. So, really, I think that takes care of all the details. By the way, when you get to Calais, there will be one of our lads from the embassy staff in Paris there to make sure the French don't get awkward!" Paddy added.

"Spare me that grief! I'm quite sure they would find some damned thing wrong." John grimaced. "Can't thank you enough, Paddy. Cook's couldn't have done better!"

"I suppose you want to see that gorgeous young lady in Cologne again tomorrow. Is that the reason for your convenient stop there?"

"Right on the money, my dear friend! Can't think of any better reason," John retorted.

The next morning, Paddy drove John out to the airfield. Awaiting them was a ground crew and the Tiger Moth preflighted, fully fuelled, and ready to go. John walked around the aircraft doing his preflight inspection, thanked them all, and climbed aboard. They handed him his two suitcases, which he stowed on the front cockpit bucket seat and strapped them down. Then he climbed into the rear cockpit and settled down on the dingy pack, under which sat the parachute, and strapped in, plugging in his radio connection. *Funny*, he thought to himself, *it seems quite strange having a radio one can use in this dear old machine.* Then he looked at the instrument panel and saw something that he had not noticed when he flew the Moth down here in the dark. Neatly painted across the top of the instrument panel in white paint was, "THE BAT." He smiled and thought, *That sod Ginger, I'll bet!* After getting started, he called the tower for clearance, looked around, gave a quick salute to Paddy, waved the chocks away, and taxied out to the runway. Airborne, he turned immediately onto his first heading, climbed to a thousand feet, and levelled off. Strangely, for December, it was a clear day, chilly, of course, but the good visibility was a blessing. As he flew along in the smooth air, he thought a lot about the aircraft. How beautifully smoothly the engine ran and how incredibly well the airframe was rigged; one could literally fly it "hands-off." It really was a delight. Because of the weather, there was virtually no headwind or turbulence, and the trip down to Butzweilerhof passed seemingly quickly and very enjoyably.

After landing, he handed the aircraft over to the ground crew, who put it away for the night, and then he went on to the mess, taking one suitcase with him. Inside the hallway, he went to the telephone kiosk and called Michelle. She answered at once, as she had been expecting the call. "Stay where you are. I'm coming to see you." An hour later, her car drew up outside the mess, and John walked out to greet her. She opened the passenger door, and he climbed in, turning to her to kiss her. She turned her head slightly, offering him her cheek, and held his hand affectionately as she did so. Not quite the greeting he was expecting, but warm and sincere enough. She drove gently away, saying, "There's a lovely little restaurant quite near here; I thought we might have lunch." During the journey they spoke in generalities, inquiring after so and so, and how close Christmas was—simple small talk. Settling at a table they surveyed the menu, chose their dishes, and sipped on a glass of wine. While they were waiting, she began. "There's something I have to tell you John." *Oh dear,* he thought *I wonder what this is all about.* She continued, "I've just become engaged."

"Who's the lucky chap? Anyone I know?"

"No, I don't think so. He's a very old friend of mine, since school days, in fact. We've always been very close. We've been seeing each other a lot recently and have realized that we've really been in love all along. He's always been so dear to me. Anyway, he proposed, and two days later I accepted. John, dear, I know this sounds terrible, but I was very torn between the two of you. I am so very fond of you, but it's not quite the same thing. Being really in love, that is. Oh dear, I am making a frightful mess of all this." John could see tears forming, and one ran slowly down her cheek; his heart tugged very hard. He took her hand across the table and gently squeezed it. Looking into her eyes he murmured, "You know there will always be a very special bond between us, and I shall always treasure the time we have spent together. Knowing that you are happy is all that matters to me. I'm sad, of course, for myself, but I shall always treasure the memories of you and the times we have spent together. I do know one thing; he's a very lucky chap, whoever he might be!"

Later he sat alone at the mess bar, sipping a glass of Glenfiddich and water, musing over events. Sadly he thought, *Best to put it all behind you. Write it off to experience; God knows what lies ahead, and perhaps it's best in the long run!* He finished his drink, went to his room and turned in for an early night.

The next morning he was up early, had a good breakfast, and called for transport to the Met office for a weather briefing and then onto the flight line to his aircraft. A long day lay ahead. The flight sergeant in charge of the ground crew remembered John from his previous visit there and was very helpful, enquiring after various people. "Your kite's in good order, sir. Saw to it myself; topped off the fuel tank just now. She's good to go!"

"Many thanks, flight. I appreciate that; see you again one day, no doubt!" John replied as he climbed aboard, stowing his suitcase. He ran the starting checklist silently. The airman on the propeller went through the starting preliminaries and called, "Ready." John flicked on the ignition switches and called, "Contact." The airman swung the propeller, and the engine immediately burst into life, settling down to a steady, smooth tickover. Calling for taxi clearance, John started toward the active runway. Five minutes later he was airborne, climbing out on a due westerly heading for Dieppe. The sky ahead was relatively clear with high cirrus stratus prefrontal clouds signalling the cold front that was just a little to the west of the British Isles. Although the air was cold, John was quite comfortable with his leather helmet and Irvin jacket. Levelling off, again at a thousand feet, he settled in to looking at the view of the landscape. As he proceeded, he noticed the subtle changes in the countryside below, the neat orderliness of Germany gently giving way to the seemingly softer, less measured nature of the Belgian scenery.

The previous day, almost as soon as John had departed Buckeberg, Paddy had climbed aboard the daily communications flight from Buckeberg to Northolt. He had been met there by George and had spent the night at George's home, and even as John was airborne from Butzweilerhof, they were chatting about him over breakfast. "He should be off the ground on his way to Calais about now," Paddy ventured. George took a glance at the window and the gloomy day outside, then commented, "Looks a bit dismal out there; weather forecast is for rain later this morning. I hope it will be good enough for his arrival at Wymeswold."

"Well, at least he's doing it in daylight. That should help!"

"I must say, nothing seems to bother him too much," George remarked.

"No, you're right there; when he's about his business, he seems quite unflappable. It's strange; when he's with a bunch of other pilots he's a different person. Appears to be quite feckless and innocent. Mark you, the ladies seem to lap that up. Perhaps they all want to mother him!"

"Well it's all very good cover for him, this chameleon act, if it is an act! A bit of an enigma, really. Still, I must say his instructors at the Manor can only find praise for him. They've never quite met anyone so nonchalantly dedicated to his work. They talk about his fieldwork in awe. Perhaps as well, really; he's got a lot ahead of him."

Paddy nodded in agreement. "You're right there; they have taken a shine to him. He's a very likeable personality; haven't heard anyone say they actively dislike him—'a bit full of himself' is about the worst comment I've heard. Of course, that was from another pilot. Touch of professional jealousy, perhaps?"

"Possibly, but the thing is, he is beginning to show some real talent for things to come. Airey Neave was highly impressed with him and considers him our best asset to date. He's going to make certain that the JIC board doesn't get to know about him, or he'll be a goner! This next job of his, at Pembrey, is going to be interesting for us all. I'm looking for some solid results from him," George said. "Anyway we've got a good programme ahead for him when he's finished his leave. He'll be going straight to RAF Hendon, where the Metropolitan Police have their driving school on the airfield, and, he's doing the full eight-week course, right up to their top A class standard."

"Is he now! The young bugger will enjoy that, if I know anything about him!" Paddy said with a laugh. "It will be interesting to see how he does there and what they think about him at the end of it."

"Yes, I shall be watching that with great interest. It should be very telling what someone outside the air force thinks about him and, of course, what sort of results he achieves. How the civilian population perceives him is going to be enlightening. Anyway, we shall have him back at the Manor for two weeks after it, prior to sending him on his way, fully briefed, to Pembrey in February."

Although the cloud base was lowering as John approached Dieppe, the visibility below was quite good, and as the French coastline came into view, he had no trouble picking out the airport, and the landing there went off routinely. As he taxied in, he saw the marshaller and a ground crew standing by, with a refuelling Bowser at the ready. Next to them was a man in civilian clothes, obviously British. *My welcoming party, no doubt!* John mused to himself as he shut down the engine. As he was climbing out of the cockpit, the rather willowy man approached. "Flying Officer Fraser?" he enquired, extending a hand. "That's myself," John grinned back at him and then shook his hand. "And you are?"

"Jack Hughes, from the consulate. Just wanted to make sure everything is taken care of properly." He waved a rather languid hand toward the refuelling Bowser, which had drawn up to the aircraft, and the crew, who were already starting to refuel the Tiger Moth. "If you'd care for a cup of coffee, we could stroll over to the tower here. But I suppose you want to go there anyway. Hmm?"

"Absolutely! I need to take a leak very soon, so lead me to it, please!" John countered. Ten minutes later, they stood in the dispatch office as John spoke with the weather forecaster, then filed his flight plan, drinking a very welcome cup of excellent coffee as he did so. He asked about customs clearance and was told that it had all been taken care of. Ten minutes later he was lining up the Tiger Moth for takeoff.

The sky ahead was overcast, with the cloud base above five thousand feet, with good visibility below as John turned onto his heading of 320 degrees, for Wymeswold. Almost at once, he was over the water of the English Channel, climbing to two thousand feet. There he levelled off, and, looking out on his port quarter, he could see the White Cliffs of Dover. Ahead, his track lay to the north of Dover, however, and he would coast in near Deal, then, farther on, between Margate and Canterbury he would fly over Herne Bay, across the Thames estuary, and make his second landfall at Foulness Island. About midchannel, he could have sworn he felt a different vibration, nothing positive, almost indefinable. He thought about it for a moment, and then realized he had only ever seen the channel from ground or sea level or thirty thousand feet. At two thousand feet, one gets a different perspective. He then mused on the old aviator's dictum that the engine always seems to run rougher over water and dismissed the feeling. Twenty-five minutes later, he went "feet dry" and proceeded on course. As he flew on over the flat, level countryside of Essex, he noticed that the wind had picked up and he had drifted to the right of track, that it was becoming turbulent, and that the cloud base was dropping quickly. *Well, not to worry*, he thought, *the cold front has arrived a little earlier than expected. Anyway, conditions aren't too bad; I'll press on.*

About thirty minutes later he was passing Cambridge, off to his right. The visibility was worsening by the minute; the cloud base was down to about one thousand feet above ground level, and it had begun to rain. Shielded quite well in the open cockpit by the small aeroscreen in front of him, he was protected from the rain, but he did feel the temperature dropping rapidly, even as well protected as he was. He was able to pick up various landmarks he had noted on his map and so was fairly certain of his position. Another thirty minutes later, conditions were deteriorating still more, and he was flying around 250 feet above the ground without much forward visibility. There had been a wealth of minor roads below but nothing distinctive; then, suddenly, he passed over a body of water below. It was quite distinctive in shape, and he recognized it from previous trips to Wymeswold. It was Rutland Water, which lies with the town of Oakham to the west, and Stamford to the east. He knew exactly where he was, somewhat to the right of track. Turning slightly to the left he passed over Oakham and picked up the A606 road leading from it, Northeasterly he went, to the town of Melton Mowbray, famous for its pork pies. A thought went wryly through his mind. *I'd sooner be sitting in a warm pub eating one of those right now with a pint of beer, instead of playing about in this mess up here!*

As he passed overhead Melton Mowbray, he turned due east to follow the A6006 road, which goes to Wymeswold. In driving rain, he eased back the throttle and reduced speed to sixty knots, well above stall speed, but allowing more time to react and manoeuvre. He stayed to the left of the road, knowing that when he saw Wymeswold village, he needed to be on the south side of it in order to line up for an approach to runway twenty-five. He passed over a main road. Good! This was the A46 running arrow straight north from Leicester, an old Roman road, the Fosse Way. He was about three miles from the airfield. He called Wymeswold approach, and they responded immediately. John reported his position. "Tiger One, three miles from the field on approach to runway twenty-five for landing. Would you please turn the approach lighting on fully?

"Roger, Tiger One, on finals for two five; lights coming on. Call the tower on channel four," came the reply. He felt for the radio control box and pressed the last button. "Wymeswold Tower, Tiger One, hopefully on finals for runway two five. Three down and welded." Then, "Approach lights in sight."

At that moment, the rain turned to sleet, and ice immediately began to form on the wings and rigging; the propeller started to sling ice off and to vibrate badly. The tower came back. "Roger, Tiger One, you are clear to land, runway two five. We do not have you visual; report on the runway." John was now over the approach lights, with full power on, trying to maintain airspeed with the extra weight and drag of the ice buildup. Then came a loud bang, almost like an explosion. The engine revs screamed, and bits of debris were flying all around him. In an instant, he had throttled back and knocked off the ignition switches;

the engine was silent. Ahead, the runway approach lighting, each one on its pole, lay before him. He was sinking like a brick. He pushed forward on the stick to counteract the tail heaviness due to the loss of the propeller, and fed in some right rudder and a little aileron, moving his approach to the right of the lights. No time to check instrument airspeed; just don't stall, and land straight ahead. Against every instinct to "stretch the glide," he finessed the aircraft to round out just above the grass undershoot area; a crosswind gust hit the aircraft, and he corrected with aileron and rudder, easing back on the stick at the same time. There was an immediate thump, and the Tiger Moth touched down in a three-pointer, slowing immediately in the wet grass. Then, another bump as it left the grass, ran onto the threshold of the runway, and came to a standstill.

Feeling somewhat at a loss for words, John pressed the transmit button and said, "Wymeswold tower, Tiger One has arrived!"

"Roger that! We can't see you, and the caravan is not manned today. Please report your position, and when you are clear the active, taxi to dispersal."

"Would that I could," John replied in nonstandard parlance. "Be advised, I no longer have a propeller, therefore cannot move from this position."

"Stand by!" came the time honoured response.

"Please send a towing vehicle and a towing arm to the threshold of two five. My aircraft is obstructing the runway. Furthermore, I am now on battery power and will soon be without communication. Please acknowledge," John replied.

"Roger, Tiger One. Help is on the way."

"Copied, over, and most definitely out!" John climbed somewhat disconsolately out of the cockpit and walked around his ice-covered aircraft. Pausing in front of it, he looked at the ragged stump of the propeller. No doubt the propeller was at least fifteen years old, had been stored for a while, and had "dried out." *Perhaps it had started to delaminate*, John thought, *then the thermal shock and imbalance, caused by the ice accretion, caused it to break up. Maybe, or could it be something else?*

He gently patted the nose cowling as he might have done with a horse. "Dear old bird, you've been a good old girl. Thank you for all the good times we've had together and for getting me safely back in one piece. I don't think we've done too badly at all," he said softly.

At that moment, he heard vehicles approaching. First a fire truck, all bells and whistles, followed by a Land Rover station wagon, and, bringing up the rear, a tractor with a towing arm hooked on behind. It had begun to snow lightly. The entourage arrived, and the troops set to work to couple up the aircraft. Out of the Land Rover climbed Paddy. John walked over to greet him. "Where the bloody hell have you appeared from?" John exclaimed.

"Oh, just hanging about trying to keep you out of trouble, of course! What else would I be doing now?" Paddy retorted and grasped John firmly by the hand. "Look, John, I thought you would be a bit weary after your labours today and probably would not enjoy a bracing ride on that monster motorbike in this lovely weather, so I've booked you a room in the mess here for the night. Okay, okay?"

"Great idea, old friend! What I need now is a hot bath and a good dinner," John enthusiastically replied.

That evening, after dinner, they were alone in the bar, and Paddy filled John in with the details of his conversation with George. "I think you're going to enjoy the police driving course in particular."

"I'm sure I shall; it sounds like great fun," John replied, and then added, "You know, Paddy, I can't understand why that prop broke up the way it did. I'd like to think it wasn't tampered with. Do you think you could make some discreet inquiries?"

EPILOGUE.

The next morning, Wednesday December 22, dawned bright, clear, and chilly. After a good breakfast together, at about nine o'clock, Paddy drove John from the mess to the hangar where he had stored the Vincent. He strapped his two medium-size suitcases onto the pannier rack, said his farewells to Paddy, and set forth on his ride home. Along his route the traffic was light, and he was in no particular hurry. The Vincent was ambling along at 50 mph, barely above tickover, through the bucolic scenery of Leicestershire, across land that had been lovingly farmed for the last thousand years. John, shielded from the chilly slipstream by the windshield and warm clothing, took in the scenery and mused over the events of the last two years in Germany. That chapter of his life, and all that had gone before, was now history. A new chapter was about to begin, and it held great promise. Dangers and excitement there may be, but also wonderful moments to enjoy, like the present one. Christmas at home with friends and family, and then the new year that lay ahead, with all its portents. These happy thoughts were suddenly clouded by the thought that his incident of yesterday could have been sabotage. *If so, had his anonymity been discovered? Could one of the Bat crew be a traitor to the secret?* Then what would the future hold?